RUTHLESS SINNER

ERIKA WILDE

eBook Cover design: Maria at Steamy Designs

Cover Photo by Wander Aguiar with Wander Photography

RUTHLESS SINNER

Dark, dangerous mafia soldiers like Marco Russo were made men, but luckily for me, they weren't made for marriage. Which made my job of seducing him so much easier.

It was supposed to be a simple undercover operation. One that required me to work in a strip club in order to get close to Marco and do whatever it took to coax him to spill his family's secrets. Our attraction was undeniable, so establishing a relationship with him was the easy part. Enticing him to share sensitive information took far more finesse.

But during all those steamy nights we shared I learned enough to take down his family. I also made the stupid mistake of falling for the enemy and now I was going to have to make a choice.

My head or my heart.

My job or my love.

My end or my beginning.

Because once Marco realized who I was and how I'd deceived him, he'd have a choice to make, as well.

To let me live . . . or to kill me to prove his loyalty to his family.

CHAPTER 1

Marco

If you asked me, my brother was getting soft.

Not that I'd ever say that to Vincent's face. But come *on*. He was the oldest, the *capo*, and he'd willingly gotten engaged to some low-level girl like Marla Preston?

Dad was having a conniption over Vincent's choice, one that I was happy to stay far away from. I was just glad that the rant wasn't directed at me, for once.

Being born into the mafia, I knew it was

kind of an insult that I was just a soldier. But after a few… disappointments in my youth, Dad had decided that was the most responsibility he could expect from me and we'd left it at that. Frankly, I thought that my personal indiscretions were a lot less concerning than my other brother, Dante, announcing he wanted to leave the family mafia business entirely, but hey, what did I know?

I should probably go easier on Dad. I knew why he was so hard on me. It was his way of saying he worried. Dante, for all his damn opinions, wasn't the one who went on benders or crashed expensive cars. He and Dad went at most topics vehemently, and usually on opposing sides, but Dante was responsible, in his own way.

I was well aware that I wasn't.

But why would I be responsible when I had money to burn and a high life to live? What was the *point* of our power and wealth if I didn't have fun with it? I was a rebel, a devil-may-care rogue, and I preferred things that way.

Vincent said he enjoyed our wealth, but for him that meant expensive tailored suits, going out to fancy restaurants, and buying ridiculously lavish jewelry for his girl. Vincent's idea of fun, and mine, were polar opposite. Although my kind of fun *did* involve women. I'm pretty sure that my fondness for females was the reason Vincent not-so-affectionately called me a manwhore.

Like now. Currently, I sat in the VIP area of the strip club I liked to call my home away from home. I liked it here for three reasons. The first was business. I wasn't exactly holding court—that was Vincent's job—but I was around for… friendly chats, and meetings. A strip club was a great place to put your opponent off their game and make it difficult for people to overhear your conversations.

Second, it pissed off Dad to no end. *Bonus.*

Third… well, that reason should be obvious. *Women.*

The Cozy Bunny was a club that catered to pretty much exclusively mafia. There were some non-mafia guys that occasionally visited the joint, but they all knew us and knew what we were. They tended to be our more legitimate 'associates' who occasionally did business with us and overall were friendly because taking our money was more important than turning us into the cops.

The place was classy, with both a main stage and several one-pole-only stages surrounded by comfy, expensive leather couches and chairs for groups. There were a few private rooms, each one tastefully decorated in a different color scheme and given a name like *The Kitten Room* or *The Swan Room*.

That last one was my favorite, done up in white with tasteful gold accents. All the white made the room brighter, reflecting the light so it was easier to see each delicious curve of the woman I was with.

Of course, technically clients weren't supposed to touch. But if you knew the right person to talk to, and had enough cash, you could do just about anything you wanted.

So long as the woman was willing, of course.

Places like these knew how to take care of their girls. And I sure as hell wouldn't think twice about taking care of any man who put his hand where it wasn't wanted. The kind of man who forced himself on a woman was no man at all, and I'd been in a few brawls over the years defending strippers against obnoxious drunks. Planting my fist into the face of some entitled asshole was another adrenaline rush I whole-heartedly embraced.

But usually I just came here to relax and enjoy the atmosphere and women. Toss back a few drinks, shoot the breeze, maybe handle some business. Being a soldier for the family meant I was on call twenty-four-seven, whether that was cleaning up a mess or handling a late-night shipment, so I figured I might as well pass the time in a fun way.

Tonight, I was on more of a personal mission.

I liked women. And women liked me—females were definitely one of my vices. And we all had our little addictions in the mafia. Vincent's was control, and the finer things in life. Dante's was... being a crusading white knight do-gooder, I guess I would say. Mine was the thrill of the chase. It was why I made a good soldier because I loved the adrenaline rush of danger and the excitement of a risky challenge.

But few things really got my blood

pumping like seducing a woman, and making her beg to be fucked.

Okay, so yeah, maybe I was a little bit of a manwhore, because the problem was… once I had whatever woman I was pursuing, the thrill and challenge was gone. So, we'd have a lot of fun, filthy sex—my favorite kind—then I'd move on to the next conquest. The last thing I wanted was attachments of any sort, and I always made that clear right up front.

My lack of commitment to any one woman wasn't entirely my own fault. Part of it was the precarious life I led. The few women who'd seemed like they could really keep my interest had backed out the moment they realized my job entailed getting up in the middle of the night, or leaving without any prior warning or notice, to handle business for Vincent that I couldn't ever talk to them about.

It was like living a double life, and keeping those kinds of treacherous secrets, which a lot of times included killing someone, wasn't conducive to a long term relationship. So, yeah, nobody really stuck around after the third interruption and my lack of apologies as I walked out the door.

It was a way of life I'd grown used to, and who needed a wife anyway? Well, maybe Vincent did, partially because he was the oldest, the family needed an heir, and partially because he'd go off the deep end if he didn't have someone to spoil. As for me . . . I was perfectly fine and happy on my own, enjoying my flavor of the month.

Enter Jewel.

It was her stripper stage name, obviously. I figured she got it for the pasties she wore. The bright, saturated tones played off beautifully against her smooth, shimmering skin, especially in the colored lighting of the club. She was tall, even without the heels, but I loved a woman with legs for days, and I was the tallest out of my family so I was far from bothered. I knew without a doubt I could still pick her up and pin her down, and that was all I cared about.

And that sweet, toned ass... you could bounce a quarter off it.

Jewel was the new girl. She'd started dancing at the club about a month ago, and

I'd been lusting over her ever since. She was the only woman in the place that I wanted, despite the hard core flirtations of the other strippers, but she was playing hard to get. Which, of course, made me desire her even more.

Tonight though—tonight was the night . . . I could *feel* it.

I watched her as she swayed on stage in her eye-catching pasties and deep purple thong, entranced by the sensual movement of her hips, the flow of her long, wavy brown hair as she tossed her head back, and the bounce of her full, firm tits. I'd fantasized numerous times about burying my face between them as I fucked her.

Jewel watched me, too, coquettishly. I'd played the long game, letting her gradually figure out I was watching her, moving closer to the stage until I was always sitting right in front of wherever she was performing.

Just thinking about having her, watching her dance, had me insanely hard.

As she worked the pole, I saw her getting distracted—her heavy-lidded gaze kept returning to me, like she couldn't help herself. As if she could feel the insane sexual attraction that had been simmering between us for weeks now. I absently ran my palm over the substantial bulge in my pants, letting my gaze trail hungrily over her body. I saw her knuckles pale as she gripped the pole tightly, her pink, glossy lips parting, her dark, sultry eyes pinned on me.

There was something definitely different in the air between us tonight, which suddenly felt brimming with anticipation and seductive promise. She'd never been overly aggressive like some of the women here, and for the most part, her smiles had always been shy and flirtatious when she glanced my way. But this was the first time she'd maintained direct eye contact and made me feel like it was just the two of us in the room, that she'd give me anything I wanted, anything I asked for. That if I dared to crook my finger at her she'd dropped down to her knees like a good girl and crawl her way over to where I was sitting at the edge of the stage.

Or maybe it was just pure wishful thinking on my part.

I knew from asking the bouncers every

time I came into the club that she'd yet to accept or initiate a private dance in one of the back rooms with any client. I'd been waiting for Jewel to approach me when she felt comfortable, instead of her feeling obligated to accept my request for a more private showing. As much as I wanted her, I wasn't going to back her into something she didn't want in return.

It was also known that some of the girls here only worked the poles and never entertained customers in the back room, and I had to accept that maybe Jewel didn't either—because the strippers who did offer *more* were not bashful about approaching any of the men in the establishment, eager for that extra cash they made from giving them a more intimate performance.

A part of me liked that Jewel was discriminating that way—that she was pure and untouched, so to speak—that she hadn't allowed any man in this place to caress that silken skin of hers, or see what her tits really looked like without those pasties covering her nipples.

I also *hated* that she was discerning,

because her standards had thus far cock blocked me from getting her alone and all to myself.

Except tonight, when the song and her routine ended, Jewel walked off the stage and for the first time she strolled over to where I was still sitting. My mouth watered as I inhaled a whiff of her scent—strawberries and something more feminine, like arousal—and my dick hardened even more, which I hadn't been sure was possible. I was desperate to get out of these jeans… and get inside of her.

"Something you want?" Jewel murmured sweetly as she trailed her fingers along my shoulder and up the side of my neck, her touch cool against my heated skin.

I tipped my head back to meet her gaze, found her own eyes in the vicinity of my lap, and smirked. "Is it that obvious?" I replied, because there was no way she could miss the massive length of my cock straining against the front of my pants.

The amusement lurking in her expression momentarily surprised me. "You want a lap dance, then?"

She swung her leg over my thighs, but I grabbed her hips and I shook my head, trying to not be distracted by the fact that I was *finally* touching her. That her thinly covered pussy was only inches away from grinding down on my cock.

But not out here.

I tightened my fingers against her soft skin, because the last thing I wanted was to let her go now that I had all of her attention. "I want you in a private room. Just the two of us." I put my desires out in the open, so she could accept or reject them, and then I'd know where I stood with her.

I knew that she'd understand what that request meant, coming from me. The women here all gossiped and talked to each other about clients, and honestly, I was glad they did because if anyone accepted my offer, they knew exactly what they were agreeing to. Some might call it illegal—Illegal was the kind of shit that my family got themselves involved in—but I preferred to look at it as mutual pleasure.

Jewel couldn't be that naïve. She *worked* at the Cozy Bunny and everyone in the establishment was well aware that more than lap dances occurred in those private rooms, with mutual consent, of course.

And nothing would happen between us without it, which was why I wasn't budging until I had her permission.

I could see Jewel swallow a bit nervously, her fingers flexing ever so slightly against my neck as she weighed the pros and cons and tried to make up her mind. Giving her the time she needed to come to her own conclusion, I absently brushed my thumbs along the curve of her waist, not missing the catch in her breath or the slight shiver of her body that made the little tassels on her pasties shimmy, too.

After what seemed like forever, the hesitation cleared from her eyes and she smiled at me. "Sure. Just let me arrange things with the manager."

Relieved, I let her go, watching as she spoke to the guy in charge for the evening, who looked surprised that she was booking a private room, and then she headed back to me, taking my hand as I stood.

"He said you prefer the Swan Room?"

"I sure do." I couldn't wait to see how gorgeous she looked in it.

Sure enough, when we arrived and walked inside, the white of the room, combined with the low, intimate lighting, offset her skin beautifully. The warm under-tone of her body with the gold accents in the room was perfection. And with the large mirror on one wall, I could see her from just about every angle, constantly.

Of course, it was a two-way mirror. All the rooms had one, big or small, so that if a customer was suspected of mistreating one of women then management could take a look and catch him in the act. I'd already proven to be a client the club could trust with the girls, so I never worried about being watched.

Once we were in the room, I settled on the small velvet covered couch and Jewel moved to sit on my thighs and straddled my lap once again, her hands resting on my shoulders. "So, tell me what you have in mind tonight, Marco."

Surprise rippled through me, along with a bit of pleasure. "You know my name."

"Of course I do." The corner of her luscious mouth tipped up in a small grin. "You have quite the reputation around here."

I leaned my head back against the couch, so that I had a better view of her face, and her gorgeous breasts. I was in no rush to end my time with her—I'd pay for the rest of the night if that meant she was all mine for the next few hours.

"Good or bad?" I asked curiously.

"Both, depending on who you ask," she said with a shrug as her hands slid down to the buttons on my shirt and slowly, leisurely, began unfastening them, gradually revealing the tattoos inked on my skin and tracing them with the pads of her fingers. "That you can be really good, or really, really bad. There have been no complaints about either." Her tone was rife with innuendo.

Chuckling, I rested my hands on her knees then skimmed my thumbs up and down her inner thighs, coming close to, but not touching, that scrap of purple fabric between her legs. "So which are you in the mood for, Jewel? You want the good wolf, or the bad one?"

She tipped her head to the left, her pretty eyes studying my face as if seeing deeper than just the surface. "Yes, you do strike me as being a bit of a wolf."

I was aware that she'd avoided answering my good or bad question, which would easily lead into something sexual, but now I was curious to know her thoughts. "How so?"

A small frown furrowed her brows. "You seem . . . complex."

Complex. An interesting choice of word.

I'd always exuded a carefree, easy going attitude because that's what my family expected of me, but yeah, there were more layers to who I was than just that laid-back, indifferent persona that I'd been labeled with. I was shocked that she saw that in me when no one else ever had.

She moved to another button, the tips of her fingers feathering across my taut abdomen as she continued cataloguing all my traits. "You're a little predatory, judging by the way you've stalked me like prey this past month."

I almost laughed at that, but it was the

truth. "And yet it took you *weeks* to approach me."

A warm blush swept across her cheeks as she tugged the hem of my shirt from the waistband of my pants, then flattened her hands on my stomach. "That's because most wolves are dangerous. They're fierce and possessive and dominant."

Jewel spoke as if she knew me intimately, and I found it all a bit unnerving.

She slid her palms up to my tattoo covered chest, along the sides of my neck, then framed my face in her hands. She tipped my head back a bit further against the top of couch, and boldly pushed one of her thumbs past my bottom lip to touch the tip of my canine tooth. "And, they also have very sharp teeth," she whispered.

I caught her wrist and sucked her thumb deeper into my mouth, watching her eyes darken with desire before I nipped on her finger. "Ahh, the better to eat you with, my dear," I teased.

She laughed huskily. "So it's been said."

"You know, wolves are also very loyal and

devoted," I added, just to offset all those other darker traits.

"To their own pack, yes." Her gaze bore into mine purposefully. "Outsiders, not so much."

Truth. I didn't know her, really, and she didn't know me. But Jesus, this entire conversation was layered with insight and knowledge about my life she couldn't have been privy to, yet I felt strangely exposed.

"You never answered my question, Jewel," I drawled, ready to leave that scrutiny of my personality behind. "Do you want the good wolf right now, or the bad one? The choice is yours."

She stared at me for a long moment, and I watched her debate the two options, as if she were at war with herself over admitting what she truly desired. Then she finally exhaled a deep breath and said, "I want the bad wolf."

It was exactly the answer I'd been hoping to hear, and I gave her a sinful smile. "That means you're getting the fierce, possessive, dominant wolf."

I wasn't especially adept at being *good* when it came to sex, no matter what any of the strippers here said. *Bad. Dirty. Filthy. Depraved.* Yeah, those were all the ways I liked to fuck. I liked being in charge and telling my partner how to give me pleasure, and finding all the ways to turn her into a mess of begging and ecstasy.

And that's what I intended to do to Jewel.

I reached up and peeled off one of her pasties, *finally* able to nose at the breast I'd been drooling over for a month. I sucked the hard bud and part of her supple breast into my mouth, catching a taste of cherry flavor from whatever adhesive she'd used as I swirled my tongue around the tip and added an arousing scrape of my teeth.

Jewel moaned, her fingers spearing into my hair, like she hadn't been expecting me to latch onto her tit so eagerly—but definitely wanted more.

With my other hand I grabbed her breast and squeezed the mound, eliciting another strangled noise from her throat, and a thrust of hips against the length of my confined, aching cock.

I smiled at her enthusiastic response and released her nipple with a soft, suctioning pop of sound. I moved my mouth to her neck and licked my way up to her ear. "When was the last time someone touched you like this, huh sweetheart?"

"Too—too long," she admitted.

"Mmm, lucky me," I growled, yeah, *possessively*.

I peeled the decorative, jewel toned covering off her other breast and dipped back down to set my mouth on that one, too. God, she felt and tasted so damn good, just like I'd known she would. She'd been worth waiting for.

Jewel squirmed in my lap, her hips undulating sinuously as I took my time with those luscious breasts. She was a treat to be savored, and I gave both nipples equal attention—licking, biting, sucking—until they were swollen and sensitive and my damn dick was about to burst from my jeans.

When I released her breast again, she whimpered in disappointment.

"I know," I murmured, giving her nipple a pinch that made her shudder. "You want an orgasm, don't you sweetheart?"

She buried her head against my neck, as if

embarrassed to admit her desires. "Yes, please."

I slid one hand into her soft, silken hair and gripped the strands around my fingers, forcibly pulling her head back. Her eyes were glazed over with lust, and I gave her a dominant, wolfish smile.

"Then get on your knees and suck my cock," I said in a soft, but commanding tone. "Let's see how well you can do, and if you're able to earn your orgasm."

I saw the slightest hesitation in her again, and relaxed my grip on her hair, giving her room to move or stand if that's what she decided to do. If she said no or indicated that this scene wasn't what she wanted, then the game was over right then and there, despite the fact that I was hard enough to pound steel.

But after a moment of seemingly wrestling with her conscience, she followed my order and settled on her knees between my spread legs. Her hands reached up, pushing my shirt out of the way, and I watched as she opened my jeans. As soon as she had my stiff cock out of my pants, I groaned in relief. Even just having her soft, slender fingers touching me felt so fucking good after the buildup I'd had all evening.

She stared at my cock, the way it curved against my stomach, nearly up to my navel, and I saw real hunger in her eyes for the first time. Unadulterated and real.

I reached down to her face and skimmed my thumb along her bottom lip, pushing her mouth open just a bit. "You want it?" I asked.

She swallowed, and after a moment's pause, she nodded. "Yes." Then she leaned forward and licked from the base of my cock all the way up to the head.

Oh *fuck* yes. Teasing little kitten licks all over my shaft followed, and I gripped the seat cushions hard to keep myself grounded. Jewel's licks became longer, harder, dragging all the way up the underside of my cock to play with my slit, and I grunted in satisfaction.

"Yeah, just like that," I praised her. "Good girl."

Even at this angle, I could see her face flush from my approval.

"Do you like being a good girl?" I teased.

Jewel's lashes lowered as if to hide her response and I took her chin in my fingers to tip her head back until she met my gaze again. "Hey, don't be ashamed of your kinks, baby. Everything's welcome here."

A playful look slid into her eyes, and she looked determined as she said, "Thank you, sir."

I laughed. Just going from the tone in her voice, you never would've guessed she'd been self-conscious a moment before. This woman was a puzzle and I was delighted to try and solve her.

"That's a good girl," I murmured, and changed the timbre of my own voice. "Now get back on my cock."

Jewel did as she was told, only this time instead of licking and teasing, she sucked my cock into her mouth properly. She started with just the tip, then worked her way down until she had half of the thick shaft in her mouth. As I watched my cock disappearing in between those slick lips over and over, my eyes rolled back into my damn head and I sank back against the couch cushions.

I tangled my fingers into her hair again,

pushing and pulling in rhythm to her bobbing head. "Fuck, yeah, that's so good."

Her hands held my hips down so that I couldn't thrust into her mouth, and also gave her something to brace against as she sank down further and further onto my cock. I hit the back of her throat and she swallowed around me, making fire shoot through me.

"I'm not gonna last if you keep doing that," I warned her.

Jewel hummed around my cock—fuck, *fuck*—and then did it again. She sped up, and it was all I could do to remember how to breathe.

"Oh yeah, that's a good girl—fuck—I'm gonna—you need to pull back . . ."

She took me to the very edge, and just as I felt my orgasm start to pulse through my dick, she released me, though she continued stroking me fast and tight in her fist. Seconds later I groaned as hot spurts of come splashed all over my stomach, until there was nothing left in me.

Panting hard while trying to recover, I glanced down at Jewel. She looked so damned pleased with herself as I reached for a few tissues and cleaned up the mess on my belly, then tossed them into a nearby trash can.

"Did I earn an orgasm?" she asked, a sassy eyebrow arched.

"Yes. That was hot as hell, but next time, I'd rather see my come all over your breasts."

Next time . . . I shouldn't even be thinking of a second session with her, but I already knew this one time wouldn't be enough to sate my craving for her. I had a feeling I was going to break all my rules for this little jewel.

Once I could get my body to move again, I hauled her up into my lap so that she was sitting sideways. I pulled her legs apart and glanced down at her soaked thong, then lifted my gaze back to hers with a smirk. "Did you get all wet sucking me off?"

Jewel nodded. "I liked it . . . and the praise."

"Well. We'll have to keep that in mind, won't we?"

I slid my hand up her thigh and dragged my finger over her panties. Jewel let out a shuddering sigh and pressed into the touch. "Marco," she whispered.

The sound of my name on her lips was sublime. "Yeah, look at you, so close already," I said, then turned her around.

Jewel blushed when she realized that with her back to my chest, she was now facing the mirror. With her legs spread indecently wide, I pushed her panties to the side so I could get right at her slick, hot body.

"Don't be shy," I whispered in her ear. Oh, yes, like this I could kiss all over that sweet neck of hers, and get my other hand easily on her breasts. "Show me how much you like me fucking you with my fingers."

I dragged two digits through her dripping folds, finally getting to see the woman I'd been lusting after for a month give herself over to the squirms of ecstasy I'd known I could give her. She was so goddamn drenched, eagerly arching and pushing into the slide of my fingers. I found her clit with my thumb, massaging that hard kernel of flesh as I sank two fingers into her slick pussy, easy as anything, and my spent cock throbbed to life.

Oh, I was definitely going to fuck her tonight. Just as soon as I made her come all over my fingers while I watched in the mirror.

I pinched her nipple with my free hand as I sucked at her neck. Her head fell back against my shoulder, her mouth open but soundless as she thrust into my fingers. My thumb rubbed little figure eights into her clit, then flicked it, alternating what I was doing so that she could never quite get used to the rhythm. Jewel spasmed around my fingers—it was all the warning I got before she clenched around them and came with a choked cry.

I loved how quiet she was, like she was so overwhelmed with pleasure she couldn't even make noises.

Jewel sagged against me and struggled to catch her breath as I brought my fingers up to her lips. "Suck them."

She immediately opened her mouth and took my fingers inside and *fuck,* I couldn't wait to have more fun with her. "Do you want to know my plan for you?"

Jewel nodded as she continued to suck my fingers clean.

"You're mine for the rest of the night. I'm going to play with you until I'm hard again. Make you come a couple more times," I murmured into her ear. "And then I'm going to bend you over this couch and fuck you until we're both too exhausted to move. How's that sound?"

She whimpered and I pulled my fingers out of her mouth so she could reply.

"I—yes, I want that," she whispered, her eyes bright, as if she were high on all the dopamine running through her body. Which she probably was.

"What a good girl," I growled, but before I could do anything else—my damn cell phone rang.

Fuck.

It wasn't a surprise. It never was. The life of a soldier and all that. But it annoyed the hell out of me. I was right in the middle of having a good time. No, better than good—a *fantastic* time with Jewel.

Jewel pulled away with a confused look on her face as I dug into the front pocket of my jeans and retrieved my phone. "Hello?" I answered.

Oh, great, it was Toby, Vincent's second in command. Apparently he needed me to cover some shipment that was coming in since Vincent would be tied up with 'the Preston issue'.

Personally, if someone wanted to off Dmitri Preston then I thought it wasn't our problem. Sure, we were technically in charge of that family, we gave them protection and all that for their loyalty and Dmitri *was* Marla's brother—*Marla,* who was now Vincent's fiancée—but Dmitri had been coming to the Cozy Bunny as long as I had and I'd seen the way he went after other men's women. I'd known it was only a matter of time until the reckless son of a bitch got himself killed.

But hey, I was just a soldier, so what did I know?

Holding in a frustrated sigh, I told Toby I'd take care of the incoming shipment and to text me the details, then hung up and looked at Jewel, who was now sitting beside me. I was waiting for the pout, the rolling of the eyes, the pleading for me to stay and finish. I'd just promised her a few orgasms and a good fucking, and now I was about to leave. She had to be upset.

But Jewel just cocked an eyebrow at me, surprising the hell out of me with her nonchalant attitude after what we'd just done. "Duty calls?"

"Something like that," I muttered, refastening my jeans.

To my surprise she laughed and got up, walking over to a tasteful set of drawers and opening one of them to reveal cleaning supplies. "Don't even worry about it," she said dismissively. "Have fun storming the castle and all that."

I blinked in shock at her flippant response. "Um. Yeah."

On autopilot I pulled out my wallet to get the roll of Benjamins. Jewel caught it neatly when I tossed it to her. Then she gave me a joking curtsy. "Thank you, sir."

I found myself chuckling. I'd had more women than I could count in my life turn me on, but few who'd made me laugh. "You're not... upset? Annoyed? Sad?"

Jewel gave me an odd look that seemed to cover up a deeper emotion I couldn't fully decipher. "Why would I be upset or sad?" She shrugged casually as she retrieved her colorful pasties from the sofa cushion where I'd left them. "We're just using each other. It's all fun and money in this business, right?"

I frowned. Why did her indifference bother me so much when that was usually my own modus operandi?

"Using you?" I shook my head, and forced a smile as I started buttoning my shirt. "Nah, just borrowing you for a little while." I wasn't quite ready to let her go, and I refused to analyze that decision, either.

"Well, you can always borrow me again later." She blew me a kiss as she started for the door. "Good luck on the job."

And that was... *that,* somehow.

What—what the fuck?

CHAPTER 2

Kennedy

I didn't let myself breathe properly until I arrived safely back home to my apartment a short while later after clocking out at the club, right after my time with Marco Russo.

Then I had a nice little breakdown in the shower.

As I scrubbed off the glitter and all the evidence of our tryst in that private room, I could hardly believe that the night had happened. Even though I'd planned for this, even though I had known it was coming, I still didn't couldn't quite believe I'd managed it.

Do whatever it takes, my supervisor had said. *We're counting on you.*

I'd known then that *whatever it took* would include sex, even if my supervisor and the rest of my team would never have gone so far as to say that out loud. It would always be my choice, officially.

But we all knew the truth. The only way I could get as close to Marco as I needed to was with sex.

As a federal agent, I understood how much was at stake. Up to this point, nobody had been able to infiltrate the Russo family to take them down. For a hot minute there'd been hope that we could arrange something with Vincent without his knowledge, since everyone in the community knew about the pressure on him to get married, but then he'd chosen Marla Preston of all people.

Marla Preston. My supervisor had lost his *mind* when he'd heard that through our channels. Here he was scrambling to find a high-enough mafia daughter that would be a

Russo equal that we could turn to our side and get Vincent to marry, convinced that he would never marry below his station, and he'd gone for a random lower-level nobody.

I had to admit I had found the whole situation deeply ironic. The lower on the totem pole the person was, the easier they were to convince to feed information to the feds. But my supervisor had been so convinced that a lower person would never catch Vincent Russo's eye, so really, the joke had been on him.

Not that it mattered in the end. My supervisor already had a backup plan in place, and that plan included me, going undercover as a stripper at Cozy Bunny. Since Vincent was no longer a viable option, they'd turned their sights to his brother, Marco . . . a gorgeous mafia made man I'd felt instantly attracted to the moment I'd laid eyes on him at the club.

Talk about a conflict of interest *and* desires. My job was to pretend interest in him, to do whatever it took to get close to our mark, to lure him into a false sense of security so he spilled family secrets, but there had been nothing fake about how drawn to him I was. Or how much I wanted him in The Swan Room tonight.

I got out of the shower, put on my comfy pajamas, and sent a text to my team to let them know that after a month at Cozy Bunny and watching Marco, I'd finally given him a private dance. They'd be ecstatic. Hopefully soon I'd be able to get some good information from him to pass along.

I knew Marco wasn't stupid and I was well aware that I had to be careful around him. That was something my supervisor hadn't really considered, since Marco was only a soldier in his family business, but I'd clocked him pretty quickly—he wasn't the same kind of idiot that a lot of men at the club were. I wasn't flattering Marco when I'd told him he was complex—it was the truth from what I'd seen and surveyed over the past month—and it wouldn't be easy to get usable information out of him the way that I'd hoped.

But I was determined to try. We'd heard that Marco talked too much in bed, and so into his bed I had to go. Unofficially, of course—the feds would never *officially* pimp out one of their agents for an undercover operation.

There was a solid promotion in it for me if I did my job well, and I told myself that I cared only about justice, but that was a lie—I also wanted to advance up the ranks. Wrapping up the Russo operation would be *huge*. Marco's grandfather had been equivalent to the real-life Godfather. His father Antonio, the current head of everything, was said to be even sharper, even bolder, even better—the carefully-honed and raised protégé.

They were one of the biggest mafia families in town. To take them down would be to destabilize the entire mafia world, and would pretty well scare shitless the other families. I had to get my information, no matter what the cost.

The gossip from the other women at the club had helped. It had prepared me for how this whole thing would go with Marco. Of course, nothing could have prepared me for actually *being* alone with him and how easily he'd seduced me.

Or rather, how easily I'd *let* him seduce me.

Pictures from my briefing hadn't done him justice. He was tall, but he was also *built*. Marco was a soldier, surprisingly lower on the work ladder for his status, but reports of some reckless behavior in his youth had meant dear old Daddy didn't trust him with the truly important decisions. Those went to his oldest brother, Vincent.

Soldiers had to be lethal weapons, every inch of them able to kill. Marco looked it. Broad muscles everywhere, thick, long fingers, and I'd known just from the massive bulge in his pants when I danced up on stage, his cock would match.

He's an Italian stallion, the other strippers told me, *in every way.*

They hadn't lied, and I'd found it far too easy to dance for him. Far too easy to slide into his lap tonight and let him take me to one of the private rooms in back.

Part of me had hoped he would be good in bed so that I could at least enjoy this operation. There was nothing worse than having to sleep with someone you found slimy or ugly. But the other part of me had hoped to be unimpressed by the sex so that it would be easier to focus on my work and getting Marco to trust me.

No such luck. His sexy voice, his talented fingers, his huge *cock*...now, they were all a serious distraction.

I pressed my legs together and set my phone aside. I know it was awful to admit, but I was disappointed that he'd had to leave before he could actually fuck me, but if things went according to plan, I'd get more chances. And more opportunities to find out information. What I'd overheard from his side of the phone conversation hadn't been much, certainly not enough to set up a sting. I needed more.

More *information,* of course, not more of *him*.

This was about the work. About justice. About getting a well-deserved promotion, and along with that an increase in salary. This was *not* about fucking a hot guy, even if the last time I'd been with someone it had been well over a year with Jared, and he'd proven to be a disappointment and a half.

I got a text back. *Good job, Kennedy. Keep it up.*

I sent a confirmation and crawled into bed. This was going to be difficult. Marco had never had a serious relationship, never kept a girl for more than a few weeks after he'd first started sleeping with her. Somehow, I had to convince him to let me stick around long enough to get the right kind of intel out of him that would allow us to strike. To take down the Russo crime syndicate once and for all.

That's what I had to focus on.

I rolled over onto my side, staring into the darkness of my room. Not really my room, of course. It was the apartment I'd stay in for the duration of my undercover assignment. My last name was different, my address, all the personal affects in the apartment carefully planned to showcase a life that didn't belong to me. If Marco, any of my coworkers at Cozy Bunny, or anyone else stopped by to see me, they'd see no evidence that I was with the FBI. My entire life right now was a fabrication, with no paper trail leading to my real identity.

That was how it had to be, but it made me feel empty inside, lying here. I wasn't really *home.* There was no sense of safety or comfort here, just the same bone-deep loneliness I'd felt for years, since those days of being shuffled from foster home to foster home as a kid.

Get used to it, I told myself, but I'd already been here a month. How much longer would it take for me to 'get used to it'? I missed being able to be my true self, I missed my own apartment. I supposed I should miss my friends, but part of why I'd been chosen for this assignment was that I didn't really have any family. My father had died in a workplace accident when I was a kid and my mother had passed away from cancer shortly thereafter, so I had no one to really miss me when I switched identities.

Being undercover had really made me see how alone I was. Especially with how kind all the strippers were. Hell, every employee at Cozy Bunny was kind and welcoming. "We look out for each other here," the owner, Jade, had said to me on my first day.

Jade wasn't her real name, that much was

obvious. Nobody at the club went by their real names. Partially because it was a strip club. Partially because it was a club that serviced the mafia and high-end businessmen who could make your life hell if they felt like it.

But Jade had been kind, told me that if I needed anything to not hesitate to ask, and the other girls had assured me this was true. Jade was always helpful.

About two weeks after my first day there, a stripper had been murdered, and that had shocked everyone. We'd never found out by whom—rumor had it the same guy who murdered Dmitri Preston had been responsible for this stripper's demise, as well, but whatever the case was, Vincent Russo had hushed it up real quick. Maybe he'd thought his middle brother, with his history of fuck ups, had done it, but I'd literally been dancing for Marco at the time it happened so it couldn't have been him.

The point was, the other strippers had rallied around one another. The club had gone into lockdown so fast my head had spun. Jade had us all escorted to and from our cars for days, and it hadn't been until Vincent had returned to assure her all was well and safe that she'd finally relaxed security.

It had been reassuring, honestly. To see that this was a place that cared about their employees.

Not that they would keep caring if they found out who I was and what I was doing.

I knew it was stupid of me to feel bad that I would be potentially betraying these women but… well, they were good women. Just trying to make a living. They were stripping to support kids, to get through school, to take care of sick relatives or earn a graduate degree. They trusted me as one of their own and to betray that…

Hey, if all goes well they won't even know it was you.

If everything went smoothly, there would be no link between Cozy Bunny and the Russo sting, because if the mafia found out that I was the one who'd betrayed them, I'd have to go into witness protection and that would be the worst. My entire life would go away, along with all that I'd worked so hard to earn at the Bureau.

I was never going to let that happen. I was going to succeed in this assignment and I was going to be known as the woman who took down the infamous Russo family once and for all.

No matter how handsome, or good with his body, Marco Russo might be.

CHAPTER 3

Marco

"What do you *mean* I need to bring a plus one?"

Of all the shit I thought I'd be dealing with this morning after staying up all night to take care of a shipment, Dante informing me from Toby, who'd heard it from Vincent, who had gotten the orders from Dad, that I needed to bring a plus one to Vincent's wedding was *not* on the list.

"Look, I don't have time to argue about this with you." I could hear my attorney brother, Dante, shuffling papers around in the background. "I'm just the messenger. Dad wants you and I to both bring plus ones to Vincent's wedding so we look like we're well-adjusted and settling down, or something idiotic like that," he muttered, the annoyance in his voice clear.

Dad had been married by the time he was twenty-five. Vincent was thirty-five, I was thirty-three, and Dante had just managed to score his dream of being made junior partner at his firm by the time he was thirty, basically getting the promotion as a birthday present. So, to say that dear old Dad was a little impatient with all three of us and our lack of commitment with women, would be an understatement.

He would often say how he didn't know where he'd gone wrong with us, but personally I thought he'd done a great job. He'd raised Vincent to be an excellent successor to the throne, and whether he and Dante would ever admit it or not, he'd raised Dante to be an excellent lawyer. All those years arguing with Dad had to be good for something.

Our old man just hadn't raised us to be

the type to settle down and get married young.

"And if you're going to find a stripper to bring to the wedding," Dante added over the cell phone line, "make sure she's a smart one. If you hire an escort Dad will definitely know."

"Because he'll make you go through my financials and find out?" I said with a snicker. "Who are *you* taking?"

"I have to go." Dante didn't even try to be subtle in his dodge of the question. "Talk to you later."

Yeah, right. Between his hatred for the family business and his crazy work hours, I'd be lucky if I heard from Dante again before the wedding.

"Watch your back," I warned him.

I was only half-joking. At least most mafia had the decency to shoot you in the face. Lawyers stabbed you in the back with loopholes.

After I hung up, I went to take care of the rest of my day, which meant checking in with Vincent and giving him an update on the shipment I'd overseen last night.

I hated that I'd been interrupted with Jewel at the club. I'd made a few discreet enquiries and found out that this was, in fact, her first stripping job, taken on as a way to pay the hospital and then funeral bills for her mom who'd passed recently. Tragic, and a story I'd heard far too many times before. Nobody went into stripping just for the fun of it. Mostly, it was a job that attracted women who had large debt and no other way to pay it.

That would explain her strange mix of shyness and confidence. She was a beautiful woman who had to know that. But if she wasn't used to this profession, it was probably daunting. I was more than happy to... show her the ropes.

Using each other. That phrase hadn't sat well with me then and it didn't sit well with me now. I didn't want her to feel used. My desire for her was real, and despite how bored I usually got with a woman after a few flings, I wasn't even close to being done with Jewel—and after being her first in The Swan Room, I felt uncharacteristically protective, and possessive, of her. I wanted *more,* and if nothing else my pursuit of her would serve as a damn good distraction from my family problems.

My days tended to be boring. Vincent and Dante were always busy at their jobs. There was a lot of work to be done when you were a lawyer or a *capo*. As a soldier it was a lot of… hurry up and wait.

I hadn't understood when Dad had informed me that I was going to be a soldier for the family. I'd seen it as an insult. But as angry as Dad could get at me, he wasn't a stupid man. Everything had multiple purposes. Vincent had been the one to sit me down and explain it to me.

"We need someone to be friends with the lower-level men in our family," he'd said. "We need them to feel like they can come to you with problems, like you're there for the little guy. You're on their side, we're not just the powerful bosses, we're also friends. We're all in this together."

Now that, I understood and respected. And I did like the guys I worked with. I was good with people, always had been. But it was… I didn't know what it was, honestly. I wasn't sure why I felt so... discontent with the idea of hanging out with the guys. Guys I liked, guys I considered friends.

Lately, it felt like something was missing. But I had no idea what and I wasn't about to start complaining about it. *Oh no, I was paid too well and had a nice job that didn't demand too much of me and I had so many friends that I didn't want to hang out with, my life was horrible!*

Yeah. I rolled my eyes at myself. Nobody had a perfect life. I'd just check in with everyone, make sure that we were all okay on the business front, and generally find a way to fill the time before it was late enough for me to go to Cozy Bunny and see Jewel again.

I didn't usually get this... tunnel vision when it came to women. I loved wooing women. I loved the chase. I loved winning them over and giving them pleasure. But I didn't usually think about them like *this,* to this extent.

I told myself it was just because I'd been interrupted on my very first night with her before I could do enough to satisfying my itch. I felt like there was so much more to unwrap about this woman, something that drew me in, layers that I could feel right there under my fingertips just waiting to be revealed and discovered.

For the first time in years I found… that maybe there was a woman who could hold my attention, after all.

CHAPTER 4

Kennedy

To say I was nervous to go to work would be a bit of an understatement. I had trained for this, and yet, my stomach still churned with nerves.

Had I done the right thing last night? Being so carefree about Marco having to leave? Had I been enough, done enough, to make him want to see me again? Or would he move on and I'd have to find another way to get his attention again? That would be painfully obvious. Of course, I had no doubt that many, many other women in Marco's life had tried to keep his attention after he had moved on. I didn't want to be just another pathetic hanger-on.

I guess I would find out when I was at work. I'd find out if Marco was there, and if he still wanted me.

I had a call with my supervisor. Johnson. The most boring name, and he often made jokes about it. *Yeah, an FBI agent named Johnson, get all the laughing out of your system rookie, I've heard it all before*. I'd always liked him well enough, even though I was painfully aware that he would use me in whatever manner necessary to get the bad guys. He'd use *anyone* to catch the bad guys. To him, you were an asset, a tool, first and a person second.

Maybe that was how it had to be sometimes, but I'd always promised myself that when I got promoted, I'd treat my agents differently. I didn't like feeling... disposable.

Of course, the men in the mafia felt disposable too, I was sure. At least we were working to help people and serve the greater good. At least we weren't promoting crime and violence. I was going to do good in the world and help bring justice. I had to remember that.

"How are you feeling?" was the first thing Johnson asked me.

"Good, sir," I told him, because I knew that was what he wanted to hear. There was a department shrink that I could use, and I knew if I said I was struggling he'd suggest that I just go to them, but...

I also knew that would feel like I'd failed. That there would be judgment with Johnson and other agents. *She couldn't handle the assignment. Just one month undercover and she needed a shrink.*

"We were interrupted, as I said in my report," I said, idly pacing in the small apartment living room. "I'm hoping to get him alone again, maybe get him to talk about what the interruption entailed."

"Good," Johnson said in a brusque tone. "Sex is his weak point, Lancaster, use it."

I rolled my eyes. "Of course, sir. That's

why I'm at Cozy Bunny and not one of the guys."

There was a slight pause, and I wondered if I'd been a little too cheeky with my reply. Johnson never was much for humor.

"You've got him hooked," he finally said, all business. "Do whatever it takes to keep him on the line. And remember to be careful. Marco might seem like the frivolous one of the three but he's dangerous."

I found myself wanting to protest that I thought Marco was far more intelligent than Johnson believed, but I kept it to myself. Johnson wouldn't appreciate me disagreeing with him and might say I was overestimating my target. But I'd rather overestimate than be caught unprepared.

"He's a soldier," Johnson went on. "He's the one closest to death every day, the one who deals regularly in violence. Keep yourself sharp."

"Of course. I know things have changed with Vincent now that he's engaged to Marla Preston and along with what happened to her brother, Dmitri, and him being murdered. I'll be careful."

"Good." Johnson hung up.

And there was nothing for me to do but hang out for the rest of the day.

I had to make my life seem believable. It wouldn't be surprising if there was someone watching me, especially if I managed to get really close to Marco and made myself his proper girlfriend, which was the ultimate hope. Vincent Russo and his father, Antonio Russo, both were paranoid men, good planners, and they hadn't maintained all of the power that they'd inherited by just sitting on it.

Sure, some families like the Petrovs were so well ensconced in the mafia world, so far-reaching like a fat spider, that they could afford to have a few members who were idiots or lazy.

But the Russos, while powerful, were small. They weren't quite as established. Three generations might seem like a lot when you consider how long people lived but a quick look a history showed how quickly a king's lineage could fall.

It was obviously why Vincent was rushing to marry Miss Preston. Rumor had it that she'd been knocked up but I'd done plenty of studying on Vincent Russo in the hope that we could find a woman to turn in time to be his bride and he wasn't the type of guy to knock a woman up. He was far too careful to make that kind of mistake.

But he needed an heir. And he needed more than one. So now… Marla.

I hoped the poor woman was up to the task.

The point was, if Vincent or his father saw that I was close with Marco, closer than women normally got to him, you can bet your ass they'd send some of their men to tail me, to make sure I was clean. I had to live an authentic life. I had to be not Kennedy Lancaster, but Kennedy Shapiro, and Kennedy Shapiro had to be *real*.

So I got up, got out, and went shopping. I didn't buy anything, although I did make friends with the owner of a local vintage shop, asking for advice on some good outfits for performing. I wasn't a burlesque dancer, nothing *that* fancy, but I couldn't wear the same basic pasties forever.

I grabbed lunch at a local bodega, smiled,

made friends, petted the cat. I bought some groceries and took them home, then inspected the apartment to see if there was anything I could spend a little bit of money on to spruce it up. I couldn't just rely on fake family photos. I wanted it to have a homey touch.

By then it was time to take a shower, do my hair and makeup, and prepare for the evening ahead. Getting myself all dressed up for work was an ordeal. I'd quickly realized that makeup that looked great, and normal, in regular lighting was simply washed out by the colorful, intense lighting at the club. I had to wear much more exaggerated makeup like thick, curving eyeliner and fake lashes in order to actually look like I was wearing any kind of cosmetics at all.

I dressed normally to walk to work—the team had set me up in a place close by the club—and then changed into my stripper lingerie and high heels once I got there. I'd spent forever practicing my walk. The kind of heels that strippers wore were nothing I'd ever prepared for, even with my love of footwear.

There was in fact a burlesque show at Cozy Bunny, one that showed early in the evening. It was basically a dinner show, and it was expected that customers would order a meal to go with the entertainment. Men would often come to have an afternoon meeting when the club was setting up, then finish with the burlesque show and dinner to celebrate the hard work paying off before going home. I'd seen a few men bring their girlfriends or wives, since the show was tasteful and fun and sensual, rather than straight-up pole-dancing and stripping.

I certainly wasn't qualified to be in the burlesque show. I didn't have the experience, and Marco never came to it anyway. He always arrived much later, around eleven at night.

I couldn't have my shift start only when he got there, or it would be suspicious, so I started a couple hours earlier, at nine when the burlesque show finally ended. Honestly? Stripping *was* good money. I was good at it —I'd taken dancing lessons as a kid and it had been far more fun than my piano lessons—and my supervisor had said nothing about having to hand over any money I made.

So… I kept it as a nice little nest egg, since the bureau wasn't exactly known as a job you went into for the high pay.

Like clockwork, around eleven Marco showed up. I wasn't even aware of him coming in the door. It just felt like he was suddenly there, sitting in front of me while I finished up my routine.

He wasn't getting comfortable in the chair and sprawling his legs out like he had before. He'd been teasing me then. He'd spent a month watching me, practically drooling over me, but carefully avoiding doing anything other than that—simply letting me know through the bulge in his pants how much he wanted me. That all I had to do was approach him, and he was all in, as I'd learned last night.

Now, though—now he was sitting with his elbows on his knees, leaning forward, his gaze dark and intense as he watched me hook a leg around the steel pool and lazily spin around it. He looked amazing, I had to admit. There was a rakish five o'clock shadow highlighting his jaw, his black hair was artfully mussed like he'd been running his fingers through it, and as usual he was wearing clothes that were clearly designer but also clearly casual.

He looked every inch the playboy. And I'd be lying if I said everything about him didn't turn me on. This was probably something I should've mentioned to Johnson. Or the bureau shrink. Or anybody. But I'd always been drawn to… bad boys.

Sure, there was some psychological mumbo jumbo behind it. Me, the straight-laced, top grades, FBI agent always dating the risky guys who rode motorcycles and had a loose relationship with the law. I'd even tried dating another FBI agent to—I don't know, cure myself of that dangerous attraction? Of course Jared had been painfully boring and also painfully inconsiderate, the kind of man who thought only about himself, so that plan was a bust.

But the fact was—Marco was exactly the type of man I'd have an ill-advised hookup with, and that might be more of a problem than I'd anticipated if I was getting turned on dancing for him.

His heavy-lidded gaze bore into me. There was no longer any of the lazy, come hither looks he'd given me for a month. Now he looked like a growl was trapped in his throat, like he was a wolf after prey. That prey being me.

I shivered at his determined demeanor. It looked like I wouldn't have to do much to convince him to pick things up where they'd been left off last night.

I finished my routine as the current song ended, and went to get a drink of water from the bar, acting like I hadn't really cared whether or not Marco was watching me. But suddenly, I could feel the heat of him behind me, smelled his Dior cologne, and paused.

My stomach swirled with awareness. Most men who wore expensive cologne... the cologne wore them, instead of the other way around. Marco's choice actually suited him.

I finished my drink, took a deep breath, then turned around to face him. "You know, sneaking up on a woman is a dangerous thing to do."

Marco raised an eyebrow. "I'm used to danger. Mind if I borrow you for the rest of the night?"

I preferred the term…*use one another*. It had a more impersonal ring to it and made me feel better about the whole… having sex with a mark kind of thing. But Marco already insisted on saying *borrow*, like my time was mine and he was just taking some of it for himself, and giving it back. Like nothing was truly being taken from me.

I wasn't sure how to feel about that.

"Handsome, if you can pay, you can borrow me *every* night," I replied flirtatiously.

"I've already paid and reserved our room," he said, giving me a smile that was pure, confident sin laced with a hint of danger.

I probably should've been more concerned about that danger element. I was seeing up close a harder edge to him than I'd seen before, evidence of the violent Russos I had heard so much about in my research of his family—but instead I just felt the thrum of anticipation.

He took my hand and nodded at the bartender, leading me back to the Swan

Room. It was the private room with the brightest lights, and once again I wasn't sure how to feel about that. I felt far more seen and exposed than I would've liked.

The moment the door closed behind us, Marco pressed me against it and took my face in those big hands of his—far more carefully than I would've thought, like I was something precious—and then he kissed me.

It was passionate, but not the kind of raw, uncontrolled passion I expected from him. It was soft and searching and sensual. It was our first kiss, I realized. We hadn't kissed at all last time.

No, last time had felt a lot more like I'd expected—rough, demanding, sexual. After a month of Marco making it clear he wanted to fuck me, after a month of him staring at me, he'd ordered me to blow him and then he'd fingered me to orgasm. That was the kind of dirty, filthy things that happened in these private rooms. Not... not this.

Being a stripper, I was one step up from a prostitute if I was being honest here, but that wasn't how Marco was kissing me. He kissed me like he wanted only me, that I was all that mattered to him in this moment.

I wrapped my arms around his neck and kissed him back. Partly because I had to for my role, and partly because, well... he was a damn good kisser. Make that an *amazing* kisser. He slowly deepened the kiss, sliding his tongue between my parted lips, coaxing me into sliding my tongue against his, and I felt my body melting in spite of myself.

Marco slid his arm around my waist, pressing me up against him, and I immediately felt how hard he was. The memory of that hot cock in my mouth surged through me, along with all the dirty things I hadn't let myself think about last night in the shower or in bed, lecturing myself to keep a firm line between me and my mark... all of it fell away and all I could think about was how *good* it had been.

Especially the idea of that thick shaft moving inside of me.

I wanted him to fuck me. Of course I did. He was sexy and if I was going to get anything for myself out of this job it might as well be a good orgasm that didn't come from my own hand.

Would it really be so bad to let myself enjoy this, and him?

Marco groaned encouragingly, nipping at my bottom lip and then continuing the kiss as I pressed myself completely against him, the long line of my body fitting against his broad, muscled one.

He really was all muscle, firm everywhere, no give to him. It occurred me that those broad hands currently oh-so-gently cradling my face could also crush my throat without even breaking a sweat. This was a violent man, raised in violence, and I was at his mercy.

All that gentleness would vanish if he knew what I was, who I was, and my true purpose here.

I must have tensed up because Marco slowed the kiss, turning it into something lighter and more relaxed. He was the one keeping me vertical right now, my entire weight on him as he held me against the door, my legs being carefully nudged further and further open by his thighs until they were spread wide and almost wrapped around his waist completely.

This was... different from the last time, definitely. It felt like he was putting more effort into the slow seduction. Taking time with me the way he would a proper lover, like he wasn't paying me at all.

I grabbed his arms, feeling the muscles there. His biceps were so big my fingers couldn't wrap all the way around them. I shivered. It was... I knew I shouldn't feel this way but it was so *hot*. He was so *strong*, how was I supposed to do anything except feel shivery and helpless all over? I was a tall girl, not every man could make me feel this way, and I fucking loved it.

Finally Marco pulled away from my mouth and moved down to my neck. He'd been fond of that last time, while he'd fingered me. That and my breasts. My ass was fantastic and I loved my legs but my breasts were a little on the small side, something I'd often felt insecure about.

Marco, though... he'd loved them yesterday and he was gradually pushing me higher and higher up, his mouth moving lower and lower down my body at the same time. He was lifting me so *easily*. I felt like my entire body was on fire with his touch, with anticipation, with the very fact that he could do this to me.

I moved my hands up, running my fingers through his thick, curling hair. He always kept it a little wild, and I'd long suspected there was no gel in it. I was glad to be proven right, to have nothing but soft, silky strands to tug on as Marco slowly, inexorably, reached my breasts.

It was nice of him not to rip my costume, I thought dimly. I couldn't afford to replace my stuff all the time.

"What do you want?" he murmured, his lips brushing over the curve of my breast.

I could barely think, never mind talk. "Wh-what?"

"I ran out on you last time," Marco chuckled. "Very rude of me. So how do I make it up to you? What do you want?"

Tell me what you were doing last night.

I couldn't ask him that. It would be far too obvious and make him suspicious, and Marco was clearly talking about something sexual. I had no idea what to ask for, though. I just… wanted him, more than any man I'd desired in a long time, if ever.

"I want you to fuck me," I admitted at last.

Marco's eyes darkened hungrily. I felt like a little lamb that had been spotted by a starving wolf.

I shivered, liking the feeling.

"Is that just because I'll pay extra?" he asked.

I wasn't sure if he was teasing or serious.

Honestly, I wasn't sure in general if Marco was teasing or serious. Most people seemed to assume he was a carefree kind of dude, at least when he was sitting with his buddies on one of the couches in the strip club. I had a feeling he wanted people to think that he was this affable guy, to not take him seriously, a camouflage for that darker, more savage man beneath.

"No," I replied honestly. "I want *you*."

I knew that I could get away just with handjobs or blowjobs, and avoid the full experience, as it were. Maybe not forever, but at least for a little while. This was risky, even with a condom—was it really wise for me to sleep with a mark? To blur lines like that, even for an undercover operation?

But that part of me that liked being in the line of fire, that was the first one in and the last one out during a raid, the part of me that liked dangerous men… it was shivering, heating, whispering to me *yes, yes, yes*.

And, well, no one was around to tell me otherwise.

"I liked blowing you last night," I told him, again being honest. "I want…"

I stumbled a little. It had been so long since I'd done anything with anyone, and Jared hadn't exactly been what you'd call 'adventurous' in the bedroom. I'd felt… crass, just saying what I wanted so blatantly like that.

But Marco wasn't Jared, and if I had to guess, he'd probably appreciate candor over decorum. Me voicing my dirty, deepest desires over timid modesty.

"I want that cock of yours inside me," I finished.

If he noticed my stumble, my horrible moment of insecurity, he was kind enough not to say anything about it. Instead he just grinned. "I think we can definitely manage that."

"Way to say it like you're doing me a favor," I shot back, unable to stop myself.

Marco just laughed. "You are quite the little puzzle, Jewel," he said, then set me back on my feet, keeping me steady for a moment when I wobbled on my five inch heels.

His fingers hooked in my panties, slowly dragging them down my thighs, and I couldn't repress a shiver. My body was aching for another good orgasm—no, more than that—a good, mindless *fucking*.

To my surprise, Marco lowered himself to his knees. He draped one leg over his shoulder and nosed at my folds. "You're so fucking soaked already, naughty girl."

"All for you," I murmured, and it was the truth.

I gasped as his warm tongue swiped at my already sensitive clit. I was wet, almost embarrassingly so.

"Oh, this is going to be fun," Marco murmured, almost to himself, and then he slid two fingers into me as he licked at me again.

Oh my *God.* The stretch of two fingers at once, plus his mouth on my clit—I moaned, my voice unraveling into a helpless whimper of surprise. I liked that bit of roughness of his fingers pushing inside me, that slight burn, and it had been so damn long since I'd gotten that kind of pleasure from anyone…

Marco pumped his fingers in and out of me quickly, deeply, his tongue tracing patterns on my clit that had me seeing stars. I felt like my spine was melting. I didn't even know what to do with my body, my legs trembling and threatening to give out on me at any moment.

My vision went blurry as he curled his fingers, finding just the right angle to make me cry out. I gripped my fingers in his hair to hold on. *Oh my God, oh my God, oh my—*

I felt myself hurtling towards a climax, but Marco pulled his fingers and mouth away from me before it happened. A small whine of disappointment escaped me before I could stop it. I hadn't been touched like this in so *long,* what else was I supposed to do?

Marco pulled a condom out of his wallet

and winked at me. "What, you thought I wasn't going to tease you a little?"

He undid his pants, and my mouth watered at seeing his thick, glorious cock again. Marco's eyes never left mine as he rolled the condom on. "By the time I'm finished with you, baby, you'll be screaming for me."

Oh, God, yes.

CHAPTER 5

Marco

I definitely intended to get Jewel properly naked, and myself too, in a bed back at my apartment. I didn't usually take the strippers I slept with back there—why bother when there were convenient rooms right here in the club?

But there was still something about her that I wanted to keep unwrapping. More of her that I wanted to explore. And there were limits to what the club could provide. I wanted to stretch her out and really take my time with her.

That moment where she'd faltered just before saying she wanted my cock inside of her—I'd seen this vulnerability in her. Like she was unsure how her statement would be received. She was so confident, practically cocky, the rest of the time, I had no idea what to make of this combination.

It intrigued me more than I should probably admit.

But first things first. Before I got her into my bed, I had to make her want to be there. And that meant fucking her brains out right here against the wall.

She'd seemed to like it rough, so I picked her up by sliding my hands under her thighs. Jewel squeaked in surprise, her arms wrapping around my neck as her legs latched around my waist to hold on.

"Oh my God that's hot," she blurted out, then looked horribly embarrassed she'd said that out loud.

I had a feeling that, given her height, most men didn't try to pick her up. They might not even have thought she liked that. But I could tell when a woman liked being manhandled a little.

"Don't you clam up on me," I told her. From this angle I could run my tongue over her lovely neck all I wanted, and I sure as hell didn't hold back. "I want to hear everything you're thinking in that gorgeous head of yours."

Jewel seemed surprised, but before she could say anything—if she even planned on saying anything—I pushed my cock into her, until I was buried to the hilt.

I growled, and my entire body shuddered against hers. Oh fucking hell, it was heaven.

She was so *tight*. I felt like I couldn't breathe or I'd come on the spot. Luckily, Jewel seemed to need a moment too, judging from how she trembled in my arms.

"Been a while, huh baby?" I asked.

Contrary to popular belief, strippers weren't sex workers. While I had a fun time working my way through their ranks, they weren't any easier or harder to hook-up with than the women I picked up at nightclubs, bars, or in coffee shops. There were some strippers here who *were* sex workers, but others just stripped and refused my payment when I went into the back rooms with them.

Jewel, being new here, seemed to have picked me as her first sex client. I was flattered, and damn pleased that my month of flirting with her had paid off. But I could tell it had been a while for her and I wasn't going to push her too far too fast.

I occupied myself in the meantime with kissing every part of her smooth skin that I could reach with my mouth. It was beyond fun to nip, to suck, to kiss, and figure out what responses she gave, where she liked to be touched and how. I was careful not to bruise her, or mark her up, even though I desperately wanted to.

When she relaxed enough, I pulled halfway out. "Hold on tight," I teased her.

When I thrust back into her, I felt like I saw stars. She was so fucking tight and sweet. I really wasn't going to be able to hold back—and I suspected she didn't want me to.

I pounded into her hard and fast, driving myself into that delicious tight heat again and again. And holy shit, did she like it—my cock hadn't been milked this good in ages.

I wasn't going to last long like this. But I'd be damned if I came and she didn't. I thrust into her completely and held it, grinding my cock as it was inside of her, swiveling my hips.

Jewel cried out in pleasure and surprise. "How—how are you—oh my *God.*"

"Fun little trick I picked up." I kissed her, sliding my tongue between her lips, as I continued to move my hips in a circular motion.

It not only hit that perfect angle inside of her, but because our hips were flush together, it also teasingly brushed up against her clit on the outside. Jewel moaned into my mouth, her fingers threatening to tear my shirt as she dug into it with her nails.

"Please," she whispered, her voice breaking a little. "Oh my God don't tease me please, *please—*"

Fuck, she really needed this. My veins felt like they were on fire from how turned on I was. She was so hot like this, desperate to be fucked properly, falling apart from just a little teasing. She needed this, *badly*, perhaps more than she'd realized until this moment.

There was no way I could deny her.

I pulled out and thrust back in, snapping my hips, and Jewel screamed into my mouth with pleasure. Her noises were so addicting, and the way she clawed at my back like a wildcat only added to the hot-slick euphoria building in my cock, in my blood, in my spine.

I was so close to coming, and I didn't want to leave her behind. I wondered, with how rough she seemed to like it…

I bit down on the curve of her shoulder and sped up even more, keeping that upwards angle that she seemed to love, and Jewel cried out. "I'm—I'm gonna—Marco I'm —oh my *God*—"

Her moans were music to my ears, and I started coming hard and fast, her own orgasm barely started.

I kept driving into her until it got painful, drawing out my climax and the shiver of *too much* that came after my orgasm started to subside. I was a man who liked to push the limits, including for myself, and I loved a little overstimulation at the end of my sex.

At last, though, I pulled out, setting

Jewel's feet back on the floor. She looked completely taken aback by her orgasm, her eyes glazed and her chest heaving with each breath.

"Been a while since you had a good one of those, huh?" I asked her.

She nodded, still looking dazed. "Yeah. The last guy I was with wasn't exactly… what I needed."

"His loss." I'd fuck her through the mattress if she'd let me. After I got her to beg for me, first.

Jewel looked around, her face flushed, as if she was now embarrassed about everything. It was endearing, and something in me… felt surprisingly soft, about her.

"Hey, you hungry?" I found myself asking. "Because I still kind of owe you for last night and I could go for some ice cream."

Jewel stared at me in confusion as she put her thong back on. "…what?"

"C'mon, you can always end your shift early, right?" Strippers tended to really make their own hours, so long as they completed their scheduled set on stage, which she had. And I really didn't want any other man even *looking* at her when she still had the scent of me on her skin.

"Um, yes?" Jewel looked at me like she had no idea what to make of me. My brothers looked at me like that a lot. "You're seriously inviting me out for ice cream at midnight after you fucked my brains out."

"What can I say?" I gave a playful shrug. "I'm a gentleman that way."

Jewel still looked perplexed but she snorted with laughter. "You're something, all right, that's for sure."

For a moment I was sure she'd say no, so I busied myself throwing away the condom and cleaning myself up. But then when I looked back at her, Jewel shrugged and said, "Sure. Why not?"

Hell yes. Just like that I was in business.

CHAPTER 6

Kennedy

He was inviting me out for... ice cream?

This was one of those things that when it happened with mobsters on TV, it was a joke. A comedy. Something you saw on a show like *Brooklyn 99*.

But here I was, dressed back in my street clothes, at one of those late-night Persian ice cream places that had flavors like rosehip and lavender as well as cookie dough and mint chip.

Ah, New York City, never change.

I wasn't exactly dressed for the colder evening, since it was a short walk between the club and my apartment and I usually welcomed the cool night air after shaking my ass for hours in a perfume-and-people-filled room. But now, as I shivered with my coffee ice cream (in a bowl, not a cone), I found my shoulders covered in a warm jacket.

I looked up and Marco shrugged. "Can't have you dying on me. My dad would never let me hear the end of it."

"He sounds like a real hard ass," I joked as I put the jacket on. It was soft, worn leather, and smelled like him. I tried to ignore the weird flip in my stomach.

"He's all right. He just worries about me." Marco took his Neapolitan ice cream cone and gently grabbed me by the elbow to guide me to one of the plastic outdoor tables.

I sat down. "Maybe he should, I am a stripper after all."

Marco chuckled as he sat across from me. "Nah, that's not the problem. A mafia guy who has a thing for the strip club? Practically a cliché."

"Well he's got to be worried for a good reason, then."

When I'd said yes to getting ice cream, as crazy as the idea had sounded coming from Marco Russo of all people, I'd hoped that I could endear myself to him, get him to like me more. I hadn't expected some good gossip on the Russo family dynamic. This could be perfect.

"Not really." Marco took a long, thorough lick of his ice cream and I was suddenly reminded of that tongue on my clit.

My body pulsed with desire. I hadn't been fucked that good in... possibly ever. I'd thought at the end there he was going to fuck me right through the wall and I wouldn't have minded at all.

Maybe he'll do all those other things to you, my mind whispered. *The things you never had the courage to ask for.*

I certainly hadn't bothered asking Jared, and the bad boys I'd ill-advisedly dated before him I had enjoyed but hadn't trusted enough to... really take care of me. You had to trust someone for the things I wanted in bed.

Don't be an idiot. He's mafia, he's your mark. You can't trust him.

"He's just overprotective then?" I asked, dragging my thoughts away from sex and back to the conversation at hand.

"Yeah, you could say that." Marco shrugged. "My mom explained it, a little bit before she died. I think she already knew she was dying even if she hadn't told us yet. She said I was just like my uncle."

"You have an uncle?" I asked, confused.

Marco shot me an odd look and I quickly explained. Shit. I'd fucked up, revealed I knew too much. "Everyone in the club knows the Russo family. Your grandfather's famous. So's your dad. But he doesn't have a brother, right? It's just the three of you."

"That's what they wanted everyone to think, after he died," Marco explained, apparently buying my explanation. "Ah, good old Popsy. I was the only one who got away with calling him that. Dante and Vincent always said Grandpa. Anyway. My uncle was a real party boy, daredevil, all the rest. Same as me. Kind of an embarrassment to his dad. You think *my* dad's tough, he had nothing on our grandfather. It was lucky in a… shitty kind of way that he died the way he did, before he fucked up really bad."

"I'm not sure I understand what you mean."

"Well, y'know, stupid doesn't last long in the mafia. And my uncle was apparently not gifted in the smarts department. He would've fucked up some deal, or pissed off the wrong person, ruined the whole family. But instead he got in a drunk driving accident and wrapped himself around a telephone pole."

I took another bite of my ice cream. "You don't sound all that upset."

"It was before I was born. I think maybe even before Vincent had been born. It's hard to feel sad about someone you never knew, someone that everyone was kind of… relieved that he died? It's complicated." Marco shrugged. "But my grandfather went to work erasing his own son from the story, so that there wouldn't be any blotch on our legacy."

I grimaced. "That's pretty ruthless."

"Welcome to the mafia." Marco sounded rakish and nonchalant, but I thought I detected a sadness underneath. "Mom said that Dad loved his brother even if he wasn't proud of him, and that he was worried I'd end up just like him."

I couldn't resist asking. "Would your dad erase you? If it ended that way?"

"Well I'm a lot of things, but stupid isn't one of them, so I won't end up that way. But if I did… I don't know. Dad cares about us even if sometimes he's crappy about showing it."

I almost wanted to tell Marco that he sure wasn't as brainless as my boss thought, but he was still spilling his personal business to an FBI agent. I kept my mouth shut and my ears open. I wasn't sure why he was telling me this, and there was enough softness left in me to realize what a privilege it was—and to feel guilty that I was probably going to use this against him someday soon.

What I said out loud was, "So you let your father underestimate you."

Marco gave me an odd, sharp look, a wolf scenting danger. "What do you mean?"

"I mean you're not nearly as stupid as you want people to think you are," I replied. "You wanted me to roll my eyes at you just now when you said you wouldn't end up that way. You like it when people underestimate you."

Marco looked thrown, but also impressed. "You should be a cop with people reading skills like that."

You're not too far off, I thought grimly. "Being a stripper pays better. And they don't complain when you sleep with clients. I hear sleeping with criminals is frowned upon in the cop community."

Marco laughed. "You're something else, Jewel. I can't get a read on you. I like it."

My stomach flipped again, this time less from pleasure and more from fear. It was a good thing that he couldn't get a read on me, right? That I intrigued him?

We finished up our ice cream. Marco stood, offering me his arm. "You live near here?"

I took his arm and let him tuck me into his side. "Why, you going to turn around and be a gentleman?"

"If that's what you want," he replied evenly. "Or... I could take you back to my place."

His place. As far as I knew, Marco didn't really take strippers to his apartment. This was perfect. This was it.

"What will we do if we go there?" I asked.

There was a part of me, one I didn't want to look at too hard, that wasn't asking to be coy and play the game. It was asking because I had yet to see him naked and I wanted to get my hands and mouth on his body, so goddamn badly. Being fucked with all of my partner's clothes on was very hot, the impression that they were so in control and I wasn't just adding to the experience. But I wanted to see the muscles and tattoos that lurked underneath the expensive clothing.

Marco's voice, when he spoke, held that growl that sent shivers up my spine. "Not sleeping," he said. "That's for sure."

I said yes.

And it wasn't just because of the job.

CHAPTER 7

Marco

My place was decked out, but also definitely a bachelor pad.

I fucking loved it.

Loft apartment in the city? Check. Huge floor-to-ceiling windows? Check. Open-plan so that if I wanted to hold parties I could? Check. Built-in surround sound stereo for optimal movie marathons or dance parties? Check. Huge California King sized bed up against the exposed brick wall? Check and check.

I even had a balcony with a hot tub. Bathing suits optional.

Vincent had been his usual self and insisted on installing an escape room, top of the line security cameras, a bodyguard rotation, and all the rest—but I didn't really care. I was just a soldier, and the second son. I had no real power, so what would someone want with me?

As long as the security measures didn't get in the way of my fun, though, I supposed it was fine.

As I opened the door, I flicked on the lights. So far, Jewel hadn't been all that impressed with the doorman or the private elevator. I wasn't sure if I wanted her to be impressed or not. The fact that she was genuinely accepting and calm about the richness of my life was… a nice novelty.

But then I flicked on the lights and I saw her jaw drop and her eyes go wide. I grinned. "Not too shabby, huh?"

Jewel swallowed, clearly trying to act composed. "Um. It's pretty nice."

I laughed. "I know, it screams bachelor pad. And it technically is a studio. But I think the view makes up for it."

Jewel sent me a playful glare as she took off her absurdly high heels and walked into the apartment. "Technically a studio. I can see why your brothers find you insufferable."

"But the ladies find me charming."

"For a week!" Jewel shot over her shoulder. "Don't think I didn't hear from the other girls how quickly you moved through them!"

"That was me getting bored of them, not the other way around." I followed her as she walked through the dark blue-and-gold color coded apartment. It was oddly nice, to watch her move around in her bare feet, at ease in my home.

"Oh, I'll expect you to stop calling me on Saturday, then?" Jewel paused in front of the windows and stared out across the sea of warm lights and apartment buildings.

Even though that was the pattern, the idea that I was so predictable… it got to me. I didn't want to be so easy to judge that this woman could write me off effortlessly. I didn't want to be just some fling for her where she knew I had one foot out the door.

"Don't sell yourself short," I said, hoping I didn't let it show that she'd gotten to me with that comment. "You could last a whole extra week."

Jewel laughed. "I'm not sure I'm quite that fascinating. Or that good at sex."

"Well on that last one I know you're *definitely* selling yourself short."

Jewel turned away from the window to look at me, her brows slightly furrowed. "You're really not how I expected."

"It's the ice cream, isn't it?" I teased.

"Yes," she said, her tone serious.

That threw me for a loop. "Well, what did you expect?"

"Someone a lot less . . . courteous." She let her arms fall to her side, vulnerable and brash in the same instant. "Someone who cared more about the notches in his bedpost than making sure his partner had a good time."

I flashed her a grin. "Well, turns out I'm only half a cad."

"Turns out." Jewel grinned back at me, and my heart felt like it was melting a little.

I didn't know why I so badly wanted this woman to respect me, but I did. I wanted her to have a good opinion of me. "If you like the view from the window, you should really see it from the balcony. I have a hot tub and everything."

Jewel pretended to think about it for a moment. "Only if you get in, too."

"Fair enough. I'll even go first."

I stripped off my shirt as I walked towards the balcony, just letting it drop to the floor. I wasn't exactly shy about nudity. Why worry about getting naked with someone you'd already slept with and would sleep with again shortly?

I thought I heard a noise behind me, almost like a gasp, but I thought it was just Jewel seeing the hot tub and the balcony until I took off my pants and turned around—and saw her staring at my chest, then my arms.

More specifically, at my tattoos.

I'd forgotten until that moment that Jewel hadn't seen me without my clothes on until now. She'd probably glimpsed the ink on my chest, but not everything. I tended to wear long sleeves when out and about, just because my tattoos were rather personal to me and Dad had given me plenty of lectures about not being 'stereotypical'. Tattoos could also link you to particular gangs, and I didn't want anyone who talked to me to immediately know who I was if they recognized, say, the ancestral family crest from Italy that was on my bicep, various thorned vines wrapped around it.

I was proud of my tattoos, though. I'd worked hard thinking about what each of them would look like and what they meant to me. I thought they were… beautiful, honestly, even if most people just saw them as another 'gangster' thing to do.

Jewel walked over to get a closer look. "Mind if I… um… wow. Just… wow. Those are really great."

I grinned and backed into the hot tub. "C'mon in join me. I might even let you touch them."

"You might?" Jewel replied, taking off her clothes. "Right, because you're so hard to get."

I winked at her. "That's me."

Jewel, nothing but smooth, creamy skin, stepped into the hot water to join me. My mouth went dry looking at her. Fuck, she was stunning.

I sat down on the concrete seat that ran around against the wall of the circular hot tub and spread my legs a little, curling my fingers for her to come to me.

Jewel smirked knowingly and walked over, straddling my lap.

Fuck. Having skin to skin like this was driving me insane, instantly. Suddenly I wanted nothing more than to get my mouth on every inch of her and slide my cock into her again, forget tattoos or whatever else.

Jewel, however, was pointedly not looking me in the face and was instead examining my tattoos.

Generally, women tended to talk about how hot they were and then just move on, but Jewel had a more critical eye. She seemed to have a more critical eye in general and I kind of liked it. It made me want to… challenge myself, rise up to her expectations.

"Most of these look like they were done by the same artist."

"They are. When you find an artist you really like… why go to someone else? Just to mix it up? If I wanted a really different style, maybe, but Jax is the best."

Jewel traced one of the tattoos—the one on my chest, of a racing wolf. "This one suits you."

"Oh?"

"You've always given me the impression of a wolf." She shrugged, taking me back to the conversation we'd had the first night in The Swan Room, while providing a few new adjectives. "Deadly, powerful, a little feral… misunderstood."

That last word was unexpected, and hit me like a gut punch. "I'm hardly the brooding protagonist of a teen drama."

"No. But you're not who you like to make people think you are, either?" Jewel tilted her head and finally looked me in the eye again.

Her gaze was dark, assessing, in a way that I'd never really seen from anyone. The gazes of people like my father's enemies or business associates was a whole different ballgame. This felt… different. More intimate.

I wondered what she was seeing when she looked at me. I hoped it was something good enough.

I'd never quite been good enough, and Dad had Vincent for all that and Dante for the simultaneous overachieving and disappointing the family, so I could kind of just do as I pleased. Why bother trying to get approval when it wouldn't be *me*? Why compete for attention that way?

But now, for the first time in years, I found myself wanting to be... good enough. For this woman.

I was sitting down in the hot tub but I felt like I was standing on the railing of my balcony, dizzy, full of vertigo, ready to fall off.

"Are you?" I asked, turning the conversation around on her. "You're a stripper. Are you exactly who you portray yourself to be on stage?"

Jewel gave a small smile. "No. Fair point." She ran her finger along the outside of the wolf before tapping the rainbow flames on my right shoulder. "What's this?"

"That was a tough one. Not any line art,

literally filling in color on my skin so it took forever and stung something horrible. But it was worth it." I grinned at her. "I'm really good with fire. It's one of my specialties. If something needs to be burned down, I'm usually the one to do it. But the reason I'm so good with it is I started out as a punk teenager with a rebellious streak. One time we were at the family lake house for the summer and I got a little too enthusiastic with this fire-eating trick I was trying. The shed caught fire. Which would've been bad enough, but we were down at the lake house for the Fourth of July."

Jewel clapped a hand over her mouth. "Oh *no*."

"Oh yeah." I nodded, still grinning. "Ten thousand dollars' worth of fireworks, up in flames, firing everywhere in every color imaginable. I thought my dad was gonna kill me."

Jewel laughed. "You were just a little troublemaker all your life, huh?"

"More like someone who didn't think about the possible consequences before he acted."

Jewel gave me an odd look and I wondered if I'd let too much slip, revealed too much behind the carefree mask I always wore. Then she tapped the family crest tattoo on my other arm. "I'm going to take a wild guess that this has something to do with your ancestry."

I nodded. "It's our ancestral crest from our family back in Italy."

"Why the thorns?"

I shrugged. "My family feelings are… complicated. I love them, I love my family, but they're also a pain in my ass. So… thorns. But also vines, twisting… you can't escape your family."

"I don't really have family," she admitted quietly. "I don't know if it's better or worse or just different."

"You could do a lot better than mine," I warned her.

"Oh, yes, I could do a lot better than a rich and powerful family, mmhhmm," Jewel deadpanned.

I chuckled. "Look my family's nuts, okay? Vincent's the most snobbish anal retentive jerk, and Dante's just looking for the first opportunity to get out, as if he's somehow better than any of us, as if being a lawyer doesn't mean compromises and dealing with shitty situations the way our world does. Dad is convinced I'm going to disappoint him. Yeah, you could do a lot better."

This was a lot more than I'd admitted to a lot of people. In fact I couldn't remember the last time I'd talked about any of this. It was hard for my friends, my fellow soldiers, to understand how I could complain when I was rich and taken care of, or why if my family annoyed me so much I didn't find some way to get rid of them and assume control myself.

If only it was that simple. But I loved my family, even if I frequently wanted to strangle them. And I didn't want to be in charge. That wasn't my way.

Jewel traced her finger around the crest, up and down the thorned vines. "I don't know if I deserve better or not, because I haven't really known you for that long. So I'm not going to give you platitudes that would probably be empty. But I can tell you that from what I've seen of you already, you're nothing like what I thought you would be. And I know I'd want to stick around to know you more, if you'd want, and that's more than I can say about most men I've met. I think you have depths. Depths maybe even you've forgotten you had."

I stared up at her, completely unprepared for this. She wasn't fawning, she wasn't harsh, she was just… honest. And open.

I wanted to be worthy of what she saw in me. I'd never… felt that way about someone before. It was elating and terrifying in the same moment.

"Well, spend a little more time with me and we'll see how your opinion changes," I joked, trying to get back onto familiar, comfortable ground.

Jewel seemed to sense this, because she went back to asking me about my tattoos, tracing the designs as I explained them. I tried to keep them above the elbow so that they weren't too obvious, only peeking out if I wore a t-shirt.

"You really take these seriously," Jewel noted.

"They're my story," I replied. I didn't know how to explain it other than that.

Jewel's gaze tracked the various ink pictures for a moment, then she looked up at me, something vulnerable in her eyes. "Kennedy."

"What?"

"My real name, my… non-stage name. It's Kennedy." She shrugged. "You showed me something… personal of yours, I figured it was only fair I return the favor."

"Kennedy." I rolled the word around in my mouth. "I like it. It suits you."

Jewel—no, Kennedy—smiled at me. "Thanks."

We'd done more than enough talking for one night. I curled my fingers under her chin and pulled her towards me. "C'mere, Kennedy."

I kissed her softly, deeply, and for some reason, it felt like a first kiss.

CHAPTER 8

Kennedy

I didn't know exactly what was happening here but I wasn't going to argue with it.

Johnson, my supervisor, was ecstatic that I had regular 'meetings' with Marco. He didn't ask what the nature of those meetings were, and I didn't tell him. Plausible deniability for the bureau and all that. All so they could later say that they had no idea what I was doing in order to earn Marco's trust.

Honestly, I was more shocked that Marco wasn't tired of me. Maybe it was because every time he was interrupted, which was a couple times a week, I didn't make a big deal out of it. I'd just laugh and say it was fine, and just go home.

Genuinely, I didn't see why everyone else had always been so upset about it. Sure, I had to be okay with it, for my undercover work, to keep him seeing me. But I was a fed, I had some crazy hours myself. I knew how it worked. And why would I object to his interruptions when the rest of the time made up for it?

Marco Russo wasn't the kind of man I'd thought he would be. When we weren't having sex he would order us crazy takeout, and teach me how to play card games. He liked watching bad horror movies just so he could make fun of them. We went out for ice cream a lot, and he didn't drink nearly as much as I'd assumed, but he had a real appreciation for cocktails.

There was a goofy, sweet side to the guy that I didn't think anyone would've expected.

And I really... liked it. I enjoyed spending time with him.

I was aware that people at the club talked about us. I was the first girl that Marco had kept seeing for more than a couple of weeks, and all of the girls wanted to know my secret. Some out of envy, sure, but others just generally enjoyed the gossip.

"What did you do?" they would ask me. "How'd you manage it?"

"I don't know," I would tell them, because that was genuine. I really didn't know why I was different than all the others.

What was I supposed to say? *I was pretty honest with him about my opinion and I asked about his tattoos?* Not exactly stellar tips guaranteed to get your man.

Maybe it was just that I was okay with him leaving in the middle of the night—or even in the middle of sex—to go and take care of business. Or maybe he'd just never had someone who genuinely believed in him before? I wasn't going to fawn over the guy even if that might've been the advised strategy, but I wasn't going to dismiss him, either.

Not when there was clearly more to him than just the playboy persona everyone knew.

Not that he wasn't a bad boy, because he definitely was.

I'd been unable to find subtle ways to get him to go into detail about his work, the reasons he was called away, or his role in the family business. He would open up to me about his frustrations with his brothers and father, but he carefully avoided saying anything about their actual business dealings. I was building a great psychological profile of the family, but that would only be helpful academically. I needed hard facts. I needed to know how the operation ran.

There were little things, though. After a couple weeks, he said I could feel free to stay the night even when he had to go out. I'd snooped around the place but been unable to find anything, so I'd eventually just gone to sleep in his stupidly huge bed.

I'd woken up at around four in the morning to Marco coming home. I hadn't been able to see, since he didn't turn the light on and I was pretending to be asleep, but I'd smelled it on him—that hot iron scent of blood.

He'd taken a shower and by the time he'd crawled into bed with me he'd smelled only of his shampoo and soap, but I'd known what I'd smelled before.

But it was just another one of those things I didn't know how to bring up.

I was sure that my supervisor was getting impatient with me, but how impatient, I had no idea until I was dancing and Jade the manager informed me that someone had bought me for the night.

"Who?" I asked.

I was technically available to anyone, but nobody besides Marco had done so. Probably because they'd all seen Marco stalking me like a shark for a month and then figured they wouldn't try to muscle in on his girl, even if his girl was technically still open for business. This club had just seen what would happen if you stole someone's girl and nobody wanted to be the next Dmitri Preston.

But now it seemed someone had crossed

that line. Decided that my profession meant Marco couldn't put up a fuss.

Why would he, honestly? It wasn't like we were exclusive. He could've been sleeping with other women the times I wasn't with him, for all I knew.

Jade nodded towards the bar, where an older man sat nursing a whisky. "Him. Newcomer, but seems to know what he wants. Probably a floater."

"A floater?"

"One of those men who goes to a different club every time. Usually it's because their reputation would be ruined if people found out they went to clubs like these. Or they're married. Or both."

I followed her gaze to the older man and my heart leapt into my throat.

Shit. It was Johnson, my supervisor.

When your supervisor comes in person to check up on your undercover assignment, you know that you're in hot water. "I'm happy to service him," I said to Jade, hoping my tone was casual enough. "Any particular room?"

Jade had me go to the Peacock Room, one

I'd never been in before done up in rich blues and greens with hints of purple, and a few moments later Johnson was led in.

I glanced at the two-way mirror. From what the girls had told me, nobody watched or recorded the sessions, unless there was an issue with a customer. "Sir?" I asked. I didn't know how to proceed from here. I'd been told not to go to the Bureau while undercover, just in case I was being followed, but I never expected my supervisor to show up at Cozy Bunny unannounced.

Johnson, to his credit, only looked me in the eye and not at my pasties. I appreciated that. "Agent Lancaster," he murmured, keeping his voice low, but loud enough for me to hear over the music. "I don't appreciate my chain being yanked around."

I instinctively straightened my shoulders, shifting from a more seductive pose to the at-attention position I was used to at the bureau. In my other life. It felt like such another life, now. "Sir, I'm not yanking anyone around."

"You've been in close contact with your mark for nearly a month now and you're telling me you still don't have anything? Time is of the essence here."

I matched his quiet tone. "Sir, the Russo family isn't quick to trust. Nor should they be. They have a lot of allies but also a lot of enemies and they just had a murder in their territory. Everyone's still a bit on edge."

"It's not all that difficult, Lancaster," he said, shoving his hands into the front pockets of his slacks. "Just ask him where he's going and what he does. The guy's chatty in bed, everyone knows this. It's why we decided to go this route. You were there, you helped make the decision that this was the best course of action..."

"I know that, sir," I said, putting up a hand to stop his tirade. "But with all due respect, Marco Russo isn't as stupid as he acts. I'm starting to suspect there's more... calculation to him than we first thought. And we're not the only ones who know that sex is his weakness. His family knows that too and I don't know about you but I don't want to rouse Vincent Russo's suspicions. I've already been with him longer than any other girl and that's going to get them concerned. I have to be squeaky clean. I can't give them any reason not to trust me when they see that their son is interested in me."

Johnson shook his head. "We're short on time, Lancaster. The D.A.'s up my ass because of Dante and some big thing he's convinced the Russos are planning. We need intel. This isn't an operation you have the luxury of spending years on. We need to take them down or it's going to be my ass, which means it's going to be your ass."

Ah. The D.A.'s office. That was the real reason Johnson was here. He had some other people blowing smoke at him because they had their big operation and wanted to be able to use ours to get it—or have us get out of their way.

I took a deep breath. "Look, sir, I will do my best to speed this up. But the D.A. isn't the one in the field, here, and they're not trained for the field. You and I know that a good undercover operation needs time. You can't act too soon. I'm going to try and get in better, start probing, but I'm not going to blow this whole thing because I was reacting to pressure from some blowhard safe in his little law office who doesn't know what we're really dealing with. All they see are the rules, we're the ones in the trenches."

I kept my voice even the whole time, but it was a struggle. I didn't want to seem insubordinate, ungrateful, or even rebellious, and I sure as hell didn't want any passers-by or people in the next room to hear me.

But I also didn't want to be told I was doing a bad job just because I was trying to do this right. What did Johnson know of being undercover? Had he ever done this? Had he ever prostituted himself out in the name of catching the bad guy?

Sure the sex was great—the sex was annoyingly amazing—but that didn't change what I was doing! He should try sleeping with someone, seeing that person naked and vulnerable and intimate, and then try to plan how you'd betray that someone. He should give it a shot sometime. Bonus points because that someone could kill you with his bare hands!

I took a few more deep breaths. I had to stay calm. I wasn't going to be dismissed as a rookie who couldn't handle herself or told I was being an 'emotional woman'.

Johnson nodded. "I understand your frustration, Lancaster, I really do. But I want you to understand this isn't coming from me, this is coming from somewhere and someone much higher up than I am. I'll do what I can but I need you to really get me something, something solid, and soon. Understood?"

"Of course, sir."

Johnson finally sat down on the couch. "All right. I'm here, I paid for the whole damn night, you might as well tell me everything personally."

"It's mostly all in my reports, sir, but sure." I sat down as well, struck a casual, chit-chat kind of pose just in case we were being watched—because all some men want was "someone to talk to"—and explained.

I sure as hell didn't tell him about how good the sex was, though. Or how there was a deep personal meaning behind each of Marco's mouthwatering tattoos. Or how fun and playful he was, how he made me laugh and seemed eager to respect me, to prove to me that he was as smart as I thought he was.

Those facts I kept to myself.

Maybe that's when I should've realized what was happening to my heart. But of course I didn't. I was too blind to see it. And even if I had… what could I have done differently?

Absolutely nothing.

CHAPTER 9

Marco

When I showed up that night, I was ready to go. I was all set to pay for Kennedy, and I figured we'd have some fun in the Swan Room before I took her for a ride on my motorcycle. She'd never outright said anything about it but I'd seen the way her eyes gleamed whenever she caught sight of my bike, and I had some plans for her involving it.

Some *very* fun plans.

But when I got there and asked to pay for

Jewel for the night, the bartender shook her head. "A big spender came in and paid for her. She's with him right now in the Peacock Room."

My throat went dry. "She's what?"

The bartender shrugged. "She's gotta pay her bills, man. You don't own her."

Few people could get away with talking to me like that, but the person who made my cocktails was one of them. "I know that," I growled, irritated. "I just… never mind."

My stomach twisted with heat, and my heart clenched. I'd never felt like this before. I'd never been the jealous type. Why would I care who else a woman slept with? Usually I was finished with her by that point anyway.

But I wasn't finished with Kennedy. And I didn't want her to be with anyone else, even if it was just for money, I wanted her to be only with me.

I sat there, staring at the girls dancing on stage but not seeing them. The other men in the club gave me a wide berth, no doubt noticing my dark mood. I didn't know what to do with this.

What could I do?

After an hour of waiting, I went home. Fuck. *Fuck.* This wasn't good. I couldn't fall for someone, could I? That wasn't the kind of guy I was. I loved 'em and left 'em.

Except...

When I got home I pulled out my phone—what Vincent called my dating phone, the one I used for women and social shit, not the phone I used for family business. I had a folder on it that was just dating apps, over two dozen of them. I hadn't logged into them once since sleeping with Kennedy.

I scrolled through my contact list. Dozens of women, all of them with gorgeous photos as their icons—photos I'd taken of them when they were in my bed and I asked them to pose for me.

I didn't want them. Any of them. I didn't want to find someone else, whether it was at a bar or a strip club or a party or an app or, hell, a damn coffee shop. There was only one woman I wanted, and I didn't even have her number.

I wanted Kennedy.

Somewhere, without knowing why, Vincent was laughing at me. I'd given him a real hard time about his girl Marla, making jokes when Vincent had insisted he was in love with her and wanted to marry her for who she was. Vincent wasn't sentimental and he wasn't soft, what the hell was he doing marrying Marla Preston for? There had to be some ulterior motive, even as he insisted there wasn't.

Now the shoe was on the other foot and I was sitting here in my fancy apartment, for the first time in my life pissed that a woman was with someone else.

Selfishly, I hoped he was ugly and bad in bed. I hoped he was a two-pump chump. The idea that she could like another man more than she liked me, even if that man was just a customer, filled me with dread. I knew I was being childish and ridiculous, but I also couldn't make it stop.

Thank fuck that Toby, Vincent's right-hand man, gave me a call before I could do something stupid like give myself alcohol poisoning from my personal bar.

"You've been calling me a lot lately," I noted. "Ol' Vincent too busy picking out flower arrangements for the big day?"

"Miss Preston is perfectly capable of picking out her own flower arrangements," Toby replied. Toby was always placid, he never let anything get to him. That was why Vincent liked him.

Well, that, and Toby's insanely unwavering loyalty. If Toby had to pick between my father or the Russo family as a whole and Vincent specifically, he'd pick Vincent every time. True trust was rare in our world. I had to respect Toby for it—even if it pissed me off sometimes. Like tonight.

"Just give me the job," I growled.

"Of course," Toby said calmly. I knew he was filing this information away to report to my brother later. *Hey, boss, your little bro was real touchy on the phone earlier, I think you should check up on him.* "We're going to need you to deliver a package from one of our shipments to a local shop. No biggie."

"No biggie?" I snapped irritably. "What do I look like, an errand boy? Give me someone to pop or an actual important shipment—"

Toby sighed. "Mr. Marco, when has your brother ever had you do something that wasn't important?"

Damn, he did have a point there. Although what delivering a package could possibly mean for our family's plans, I didn't know. "All right. Fine. I'll be there."

I got the details from him and hung up. Fuck, this whole thing with Kennedy was putting me in a sour mood. I couldn't afford that. I couldn't afford distractions on my job, or more friction with my brothers. Something had to be done.

I had to make Kennedy mine.

CHAPTER 10

Kennedy

When I walked down the alley the next evening to get into work through the back entrance, Marco was standing there.

He leaned against the brick wall, looking the picture of danger in his black leather jacket and sunglasses.

My heart skipped a beat. Had he found me out? Was he going to kill me here in the alley, just as someone had killed that other stripper?

When Marco saw me, he took off the sunglasses, his eyes slowly taking in my attire. "Hey, baby, you look good."

That was… probably not what he would've opened with if he was planning to kill me. "Thanks." I was just wearing jeans and a sparkly pink tank top, nothing too special.

Marco hooked his sunglasses into the collar of his shirt. "I heard you had another customer last night."

"Yeah, some floater businessman." I shrugged nonchalantly. "Nothing special."

"Hmm." His eyes flashed with some kind of emotion—jealousy?—then it was gone. "I have to admit, I wasn't pleased to come in and find you already occupied."

I shrugged, trying to keep things casual. "Them's the breaks. It's my job, the guy paid for the whole night, a girl's gotta eat."

The corner of his sensual lips twitched with a semblance of a smile. "What if you didn't, though? Have to eat?"

I stared at him in confusion. He couldn't possibly be saying what I thought he was. "What do you mean?"

"You can strip, I don't mind. But I realized that I very much… do mind you sleeping with someone else." His gaze held mine intently. "So I'm asking, if I set up an arrangement with you… if you'll be exclusive. Just for me."

I blinked at him in surprise. That had been the last thing I'd expected to hear. "So I'll just be like one of the strippers that works here, but doesn't go into the backrooms, doesn't offer any off-the-menu extras."

He nodded succinctly. "Exactly."

Well, to be honest, I would be glad that I wouldn't have to ward off anyone else offering to pay for me—not that anyone had since Marco had staked a claim the first day I'd started working at Cozy Bunny. And my supervisor's visit, and purchase of my evening, had just been an anomaly.

But… "Why are you offering me this?" I tilted my head at him and put my hands on my hips. "Marco Russo, playboy extraordinaire, mad that a woman is with someone else? Doesn't seem very fair."

"Y'know, I told myself that, too." Marco stepped closer to me and I was again reminded of how damn big and strong he was, how he was basically a wall of muscle. "I told myself that I couldn't expect you to give up your job, or be exclusively mine if I was with other women. And that's when I realized I wanted this to be mutual. I haven't been with anyone else since you and I don't think I want to."

"Careful," I said, my voice coming out softer than I wanted it to, even while my heart was racing. "You sound like you actually want to date me, Marco, and everyone knows that Marco Russo doesn't do that."

"Well maybe he should." Marco smiled at me, and I could tell he was going for a smirk, but it ended up too vulnerable for that. "What do you say, Kennedy, you want to go steady?" he said playfully.

I laughed, my heart stuck in my throat. *This is a good thing,* the logical part of my brain asserted. *He trusts you. This is what your supervisor wanted. This is what you need.*

Yeah, but somehow, it felt like more than that.

For a wild, reckless second, I wanted to tell him. To confess that I was a mole, an FBI agent, and that the D.A. was building a case against his family. Maybe—it wasn't too late or too early—he would believe me and support me instead of killing me.

But that was a ridiculous thought, and I let it go. I was in this and there wasn't going to be a way to back out—not without putting a target on my back for my betrayal.

"Okay," I said. "I'll tell Jade I'm not doing the side gig anymore. Strictly stripping from now on. How's that sound?"

"Sounds like I'll pick you up after your shift," Marco replied with a huge grin. "I have plans for us."

He stepped up to me, his hands gently taking me by the elbows as he leaned in. I kissed him automatically, without thinking about it, because of course I did. I was so used to kissing him by now—and that should've been another warning, another red flag.

Marco kissed me softly, like it was a promise. "I'll see you later," he whispered as he pulled away.

"See you later," I replied.

When I got to the dressing room, I used

my burner phone to text Johnson. *He asked me to be his girlfriend, so I'm getting closer.*

The response was immediate. *Excellent. Now get us intel.*

Yada, yada, all work no play, no rest for the wicked.

I hid the phone away again and went out to do my routine. It was fun in a way, dancing and showing myself off, knowing that I was gorgeous enough to get men drooling and tossing their cash onto the stage. But the whole time I was just thinking about Marco. What he'd have planned. What I should be planning.

I was the first woman he'd liked enough to want to properly date, the first woman who'd held his attention for more than a few days, more than one or two nights. I… I didn't know how to feel about that. I should feel flattered—and I did. But that was part of the problem. Was it only because I was that good at manipulating him? Or was I really that special?

To my shame, I wanted to be that special to Marco. I wanted to be the woman that he relinquished all others for, no matter how stupid I knew that sounded. I shouldn't care that he wanted me. I shouldn't care to feel special and meaningful but—I did. I hadn't been significant to anyone since my mom died, the last person who'd truly been close to me. I wanted to be that special to someone again.

None of it's real, I told myself ferociously as I finished up for the evening and went to the back room to freshen up and change back into my street clothes.

Well, for me it wasn't real because of my deceit. But Marco didn't know that. The situation was real for him. Was I that special to him? And if I was—could I find it in myself to completely betray someone who cared about me like that?

Marco was waiting when I stepped back out into the alley, only this time he was leaning against his motorcycle.

Oh, my God. I knew he had one but we'd never ridden it together. My legs trembled, my body already getting hot at the thought of that machine between my thighs, molded to Marco's back as we rode...

"Nice ride," I said, walking over and

running a hand along the leather seat. "Where are we going?"

"Just a little place I know," Marco said, and tossed me a helmet.

I put it on, and didn't bother asking if he was going to wear one, because clearly he wasn't. I shook my head. "Y'know, I can see why your dad worries about you."

Marco just smirked, swung his leg over the seat, and straddled the bike. "Hop on."

"I hope you're not trying to impress me," I warned him as I slid behind him and wrapped my arms around his waist, "because the opportunity to do that passed about a month ago."

That was a total lie. I was definitely impressed by the motorcycle and I was prepared to be impressed by whatever else he had planned, but there was no way I was going to let him know that. I didn't want him to think I was easy. Even though it had already been a month and I could probably let myself relax by this point.

Still, the thrum of arousal and anticipation that shot through me as he hit the throttle was unreal. I held on tightly and pressed my face to the back of his shoulder as we took off, out of the alley, onto the deserted late-night street.

Wherever he was taking me, I knew I'd like it. For all his fancy toys, Marco didn't like to make a big deal of things. He wasn't about taking me out to a fancy restaurant. Instead he took me to his favorite random ice cream shop. I liked that. I was ready for the low-key thing he had planned.

And in the meantime, I *really* loved pressing myself against him as we rode this motorcycle. I could feel his back muscles shifting and flexing underneath me, the firm feel of his abs against my hands as I kept my arms wrapped around him. When I rested my cheek against his back, his body sheltered me from the wind, so I could just watch the flurries of blurred light as we sped past buildings and out of the city.

I had no idea where we were going. It occurred to me, belatedly, that this could've been a setup to get me alone and out of NYC, somewhere remote, where Marco could kill me. But I had no reason to suspect I'd been found out. There was no reason to panic until then. And his jealousy earlier… surely he wasn't *that* good of an actor.

At last we stopped at a hilly park that was high up, and had a great view of the bay. Marco stopped the motorcycle and got off, offering me his hand.

"Never took you for the gentleman type," I teased him, but I took his hand anyway. It was warm and strong. I liked the way it made me feel grounded.

"I thought women liked gentlemen?"

"To a certain extent." I looked around. "Why are we here?"

Marco rubbed at the back of his neck, like he was nervous. Big bad Marco Russo, nervous? The idea was endearing.

"This is one of the areas my family bought outside of the city," he explained. "One of the ways we maintain our strength in the mafia and the legitimate business world is focusing on charity efforts. It gives us a good reputation with people, helps us with our public image. Vincent's new wife, she'll pick her own charities she wants to work with, where her focus is, but my mom was all about community outreach and the environment so she built a lot of parks. Like this one."

He gestured towards a sign I hadn't noticed before. It dubbed the place *Marco's Park* and below it had a few lines explaining who built the park and in what year.

I looked at him in surprise. "This one's yours?"

"Yeah, we all have one. Mom liked to name them after people in her life. And I think she knew that we all needed a place to go and breathe. I don't know if Vincent goes to his park a lot, but I like to come here when I need to get out of the city and just chill."

"But you love the city." New York City was vibrant, pulsing with life, and so was Marco.

"Most of the time." Marco leaned back against his motorcycle and looked out over the city, its lights gleaming like so many fireflies. "But what I do for the family… I see the dirty side of the city. The grime, the blood, the ugly. Sometimes I gotta get out and take a few deep breaths away from it all."

"I understand," I said softly. Working in the FBI wasn't the glamorous catching of bad guys like you saw on television. A lot of the time I didn't know if we were really the good guys or if there were only shades of gray. "Thank you for bringing me here."

Marco gave me a small, soft smile, and it tugged at my heart.

"Who knew the bad boy with a motorcycle had such a soft side?" I added, trying to ignore that feeling in my chest and hoping to get myself back onto safer emotional ground.

"Hey, I've got layers," Marco protested with a smirk. "And you can't say you don't like the motorcycle. I saw your face light up when you saw it."

"Well," I admitted, feeling there was no harm in telling him, "I've always had a bit of a thing for bad boys."

"Congratulations then, you hit the jackpot." He winked at me. "You ever ridden one yourself?"

"A motorcycle? No, just tandem."

"Well c'mere then." Marco patted the seat.

I laughed. "Are you going to teach me to ride it?"

"Why not?"

"It's one in the morning."

"Exactly, night's still young."

I slung my leg over and settled onto the seat of the motorcycle. "This is probably a terrible idea."

"People keep saying that when I introduce them to my ideas," Marco said, faking a thoughtful voice.

I leaned forward to get a better look at the dash, my hips rotating—right as Marco turned on the motor.

Vibrations shot right up against my clit and I gasped. I couldn't help it.

Marco stared at me for a moment in confusion—not as if he didn't know what had just happened, but like he wasn't sure if what he had seen was *actually* what he saw or if he was just imagining it.

His hand tightened on the throttle and he revved the engine.

"Oh *fuck*," I gasped out, as powerful vibrations rippled right up against my clit. With the way I was leaning forward, I'd tilted my hips at just the right angle to get all that power against my pussy, even through my jeans, like I was using a goddamn Magic Wand.

A devilish look slid over Marco's face and he revved the engine again. I moaned, squirming against the vibrations. "Marco…"

"Fuck, this is really doing it for you." He slung his leg over the seat himself, slotting in behind me and pressing himself up against my back, one arm around my waist to pin me to him.

His other hand stayed on the throttle.

"I wonder…" he mused into my ear, "could you come like this?"

"I—I don't—" He revved the engine again and I moaned, my hips shifting in a not-quite-thrust against the leather seat.

"That's it, baby, grind down." Marco kept the engine running but didn't open the throttle, keeping the vibrations at a lower, teasing hum.

A part of me felt ridiculous for getting off using a goddamn motorcycle, of all things, but I ground down against the seat, biting my lip and humming in pleasure as the vibrations continued against my clit. It really did feel good, *so* good, and Marco's body against mine, the feeling of being held in place, only added to it.

Would he hold you in place more? The dark, treacherous part of my mind whispered to me. *He'd give you what you want, if you just asked...*

I couldn't ask, I didn't know how to ask, and the idea that we'd do what I wanted and then we'd be facing each other in court, my embarrassing sexual fantasies easily brought up as a way to humiliate me...

But he *would* do so well at it. He'd give me what I craved, what I hadn't trusted other men with or knew they couldn't deliver on.

Marco nipped at the side of my neck. "Focus, baby, rock those hips for me."

I yanked myself back to the present and whimpered as Marco's hands fit themselves around my hips, guiding me into grinding down against the motorcycle seat again. I wasn't sure what turned me on more—the vibrations themselves or Marco controlling my body. His power and control were intoxicating.

I grabbed onto his arms, just to have something to hold on to as I ground down against the pulsing sensations, gasping, arching… it felt good, it felt amazing, but I didn't think… *oh God…*

"Marco," I moaned. "Marco, I can't—it's not enough, I need—fuck, please, your fingers, your cock, *something…*"

"You sure?" he teased. His lips brushed against the soft skin behind my ear. "Because you seem to be doing so well on your own…"

He revved the engine again and my eyelids fluttered, my vision blurring. I was so wet, so desperate, but I needed a more specific touch, I needed *more.*

"Please," I whispered. "Marco, please, *please.*"

"Please what?"

The bastard. "Please fuck me."

Being made to say it out loud sent a thrill through me. Marco chuckled and kissed slowly down my neck, leaving me panting desperately. "You'll want to take off your pants and bend over."

It took me a moment to understand what he was saying. Then it hit me—if he fucked me from behind, I could still be pressed against the seat of the motorcycle, using the handles for balance, and get his cock and the vibrations both.

Oh God, I was so fucking wet at the thought that I could feel it start to slide down my skin and soak the inside of my jeans.

I stood up, my legs wobbly, and got off the motorcycle so that I could strip my jeans and panties off. I was glad we were really in the middle of nowhere—there were houses, but all on the other side of the park, probably because any on this side would've spoiled the amazing city view. Between the distance and the trees, we were pretty safe from any prying eyes at the windows. And who was going to be in a park this late anyway?

I didn't dare look at Marco. I had imagined being this bold before, but I'd never actually done anything like this. I'd channeled any wildness into my straitlaced job, took that boldness and made it about enforcing the rules instead of breaking them. I didn't know what would happen if I looked at him, what kind of creature I was unleashing—not in Marco, but in myself.

As soon as I was situated on the seat in front of Marco again, he slid his hand up my back and guided me down, so that I was now folded forward, my hands braced on the handles of the motorcycle and my cheek resting on the cool steel of the gas tank. His hands moved to my hips, gently tilting them, and then I felt cool, slick fingers sliding down between my folds. My breath hitched, the motorcycle thrumming beneath me, keeping me on edge.

My fingers tightened around the handles as he twisted two fingers into me. I was so wet, so keyed up, that they sank in absurdly easy, a slick sound that had me shivering with the debauchery of it.

God he was so good at this, knew my body so well by this point, his fingers scissoring, curling, making sure I was stretched and ready for him. The vibrations thrummed through me the entire time, never letting up, keeping me right on edge. At this point I felt almost certain that I'd orgasm the second Marco so much as nudged the head of his cock inside of me.

My knuckles were pale, the bones standing out against my skin as I gripped the handlebars even tighter. "Marco... *please...*"

His fingers slid out of me, and I heard his zipper being drawn down. Heat shot through me at the sound. I felt like I could hardly breathe with how hot this scenario was, how full of anticipation I was at the thought of him fucking me on his bike.

There was the crinkle of a condom wrapper, and then a moment later he lifted my hips a bit, giving him the leverage he needed to push his shaft into me.

My throat closed up and all I managed was a high, soft whine as he pushed me back down to the bike again and my entire bare pussy and clit were pressed against the vibrations. I was rather quiet during sex, the noise and breath stolen right out of me when I was really turned on, but thankfully, Marco didn't seem to mind. I knew it had bothered Jared, who'd thought it was a sign he wasn't good enough no matter how much I assured him I was getting off. But honestly, he rarely accomplished that goal.

But Marco never made a comment, didn't seem bothered by it. Even now, he just pressed soft, sucking kisses to my neck as he inched his way inside of me, stretching me and filling me bit by bit until I felt sure I would shake apart.

With this position, as Marco had guessed, I was completely bent over against the vibrating seat of the motorcycle, dominated by his body behind mine, and we were both balanced so that neither of us would fall off. This bike was built for someone even taller than I was, so my feet didn't quite touch the ground, but Marco's did and it kept him stable and able to brace for his thrusts.

The idea that my feet couldn't touch the ground, that I was helpless and at his mercy… it sent a hot thrill through me that was unmatched by just about anything.

Marco's hips became flush with mine, and to my surprise he didn't pull out to thrust back in again. Instead, he ground his hips against my ass, keeping his cock fully sheathed inside me.

My mouth fell open on a soundless moan as he reached up and revved the engine again. Oh my *God*. Oh God oh God oh God. He was stretching me, grinding at that sweet angle inside of me, the vibrations were—oh my *God*—

"So tight," Marco grunted. "Fuck, yes, baby, clench around me just like that. *Fuck.*"

I hadn't even realized I'd been doing that. I was shaking with desire, with pleasure, everything too much, so much—

Marco started to give short, sharp little thrusts that still kept him mostly inside of me —his teeth sank into my neck—he throttled the engine again—

Ohhh my *God.* I squirmed helplessly against the vibrating seat, against Marco's cock, as I came everywhere, my whole body shaking. I swore my vision went white, and if my throat hadn't strangled itself closed I would've screamed obscenely.

The vibrations didn't stop. They just kept up, against me, and Marco thrust a little harder, pulling out a little more, and it dragged my orgasm out. I wanted to scream that it was too much, *oh God,* I couldn't handle so much pleasure, but I had no voice for it, I could only writhe in his grip and ride it out until at last he came with deep, guttural grunts, then finally turned off the engine, allowing my orgasm to finally fade.

Holy fuck. I had never come that hard, or

for that span of time, in my life. I hadn't even known an orgasm could last that long. I was shaking so hard I worried I might fall off the bike if it wasn't for Marco's hands keeping me steady.

"I hope you brought something to clean us up with," I said shakily.

Marco laughed gruffly. I turned to look at him over my shoulder. His face was flushed, his hair mussed. He was just as sexy after sex as any other time. "I come prepared."

"Because you're a gentleman?"

"Maybe. Or maybe because I'm the kind of guy who'll have sex anywhere and learned to carry supplies."

I turned my head and smirked at him. "Hmm, which one of those is more likely?"

From a compartment on the bike, he retrieved a small package of wipes. Marco did clean me up like a gentleman, though, thoroughly and softly. It made my heart swell. How he could switch from rough and dominant to sweet and thoughtful—my head spun with...

Confusion. I told myself it was just confusion and that I was overwhelmed from the hormones, from my orgasm. That was all.

"Your underwear and jeans are ruined," he pointed out as I winced in pulling them back on.

Yeah, these needed to get thrown in the laundry.

"Do you have a washer at your place?" he asked.

"Not really." I had to use the local laundromat.

"Come back to mine, then," he said, gently tucking loose strands of hair behind my ear. "Stay the night. I've got all the amenities."

"Really? You do? I hadn't noticed." I grinned at him.

Marco rolled his eyes fondly at me and then pulled me in, kissing me. "Stay the night, Kennedy."

I couldn't help but feel warm all over, thinking about how he wanted me to stay. "Of course."

I didn't think about how I'd stay every night with him, if he'd let me.

CHAPTER 11

Marco

I planned for Kennedy and me to have a nice shower to clean up, then fall into bed and sleep in the next day. I knew she worked the following evening but her shift didn't start until around eight so no reason for either of us to be up early.

It was nearly two in the morning by the time we rolled in, and all I wanted to do was clean myself up and collapse into bed with my girl.

But my damn fucking phone rang.

"What do you mean you need me to deliver a fucking package?" I snapped at Toby.

Kennedy, half undressed on her way to the shower, raised an eyebrow at me.

"Do you have any idea what time it is?" I added, even though I knew that Toby was well aware of the time.

I didn't understand what the hell my brother was playing at. Or Dad, since he was probably involved in whatever this scheme was, too. You needed me to take care of a late-night shipment coming in? Understandable. You wanted me to take out some idiot who'd seen too much or flapped his jaw at the bar? Not a problem. I was happy to do late-night runs when they were actually fucking necessary.

But a package? This couldn't wait until tomorrow? *Late* tomorrow?

Toby sighed. "Marco, you and I both know that your brother and your father don't do things without a great deal of thought. We need someone we can trust on this and I would suggest you take the late hour as a sign of how important and urgent it is rather than an attempt to piss you off. I'll text you the information."

Nowhere in his sentence was there a chance for me to say no or refuse. As if I would ever try to. I'd been born into this world and this family. I knew you didn't say no to your *don*.

I hung up and looked over at Kennedy. "I have to go."

She nodded. "Are you okay?"

"Irritated as fuck but fine," I grumbled. "I should be back soon."

She didn't seem at all upset, and even kissed me on the cheek as if she was trying to reassure me. I still didn't understand how she could be so nonchalant about my up and leaving at all hours of the night. Did it truly not rattle her?

I entertained myself with thoughts of Kennedy on my bike as I went to pick up the package. Fuck, she'd been so damn sweet and tight. And the way the vibrations had gotten to her—she'd been grinding on that bike like an animal, an almost drugged look in her gaze. And how she'd reacted when I'd manhandled her… fuck. I wondered…

For all my fun with women, there were some things I didn't get to do as much as I would've liked simply by being a son of the Russo family. Most women, if they knew, liked the thrill but there was still that… well. If you're a big tough guy covered in tattoos and you told a woman you'd like to tie her up, a lot of women get concerned, and who could blame them? How were they supposed to know if I was a good guy or not, when abusive assholes were so good at acting like good guys right up until it was too late?

But Kennedy… could I ask her? Would she be into that? Would she want every part of me, from the vulnerable parts that I was still oddly uncomfortable with to the darker parts that I tried to hide from my other flings?

Not that Kennedy was just a fling. I could admit that to myself, at least. I wasn't quite sure what she was to me, but she was sure a hell of a lot more than that.

I rolled up to the back of the post office where I was told I'd be handed the package. It was a smaller box, they all had been, and I couldn't help but wonder if maybe there were ears or fingers inside them. But the packages never felt cold, and body parts were generally sealed and then put on ice to preserve them.

Hmm.

Getting the package went off without a hitch, but once it was in my possession and I walked back to my bike, two men appeared out of the shadows as if from nowhere.

It was annoyingly dark, but I could tell by their jackets that they weren't Yakuza. Our Japanese rivals like to announce their identities with their tattoos. Not loud or crazy enough to be Irish, and most of them were up in Boston hoarding the city like dragons, anyway. I doubted any of the Italian families had turned on us.

Most likely Russian, then.

There were no words, no warning, just two men emerging from the shadows as if made of smoke.

I really hoped this package wasn't full of breakable shit.

The one on my right lunged forward with his right arm, down towards my stomach, and I dropped the package and dodged. It was only after I moved that I saw the gleam of the knife in the moonlight, the one I'd already known would be there. I swung my elbow up and caught the guy neatly on the nose, the angle perfect to shove it back against his skull and break it with a nice *snap*.

The other guy, as I'd suspected, dove for the package. I grabbed him by the ears and smashed his face into my knee.

Now that they were both reeling, I grabbed the package and dashed for my bike. Nobody could catch me when I was on that thing.

The first guy had recovered enough—faster than I'd expected—and I felt a stab of pain as something embedded itself in my shoulder. Guy could fucking throw knives?

Thank Christ he was a lousy shot, though, or maybe I was just moving fast enough. I was sure he'd been aiming for the back of my neck.

I swung onto my bike and did the thing they never expected: I headed straight for them.

Guy number two with the smashed face dove out of the way, but his companion dove *for* me, trying to tackle me off my bike. I swerved, lowered my weight down and to the side, and caught him with the back wheel, sending him sprawling.

Fuck. I wasn't sure if I should've tried to kill 'em both, but if these two were good enough to get the jump on me in the first place then it probably wasn't wise to stick around and try to make a point. I could've circled around and fired on them with my gun, but Dad had drummed in all of us that guns were always a last resort, thanks to ballistics and also how damn noisy they were. If I fired, I'd wake up the whole neighborhood.

And whatever Vincent was up to, he obviously wanted secrecy.

My shoulder ached like a motherfucker, but I gritted my teeth and ignored it as I drove to my destination. I headed a couple of false ways just to shake off any tail I had, but still made pretty good time.

The owner of the Chinese restaurant who was picking up the package looked at me in alarm when he saw the knife still stuck in my shoulder. He gestured at it and said something quietly in Chinese, but I shook my head. Vincent and Dante were always getting after me to learn other languages but they just never stuck in my head.

"I'm fine," I told him, shrugging off his attempts to help me. I needed to get out of here and get to safety. I'd delivered the package, now my job was done.

The old guy looked at me dubiously, but accepted the package and closed the door. He was probably muttering to himself about kids these days.

Christ, I had to deal with this fucking shoulder. The smart thing to do would've been to show up at Vincent's and report to him while he had one of our docs stitch me up, but that was the last thing I wanted.

I just wanted home. And Kennedy.

The wound was in the back of my shoulder but I figured a mirror would do the trick. I'd get back, stitch myself up in the bathroom, and fall asleep with Kennedy in my arms. I could report to my brother in the morning.

When I got back, I slipped in quietly, keeping the lights off. Kennedy had always slept through my entrances before, so I expected it to be more of the same—but then my damn arm gave out on me and I was hit by a wave of dizziness.

I stumbled, grabbing onto the wall for support, and the light by the bed flicked on.

Kennedy stared at me. Her skin glowed in the soft, warm lighting, but as beautiful as she was, it couldn't distract me from the alarmed look in her gaze.

She didn't remark on the fact that my shirt was covered in blood from the two guys whose noses I'd smashed. Instead she said, "I don't know if you've noticed but there's a knife in your back."

"In my shoulder," I corrected with a grunt of pain.

Kennedy winced and got up, grabbing one of the silk dressing gowns I'd bought her.

"Let me see that," she said, her hands firm but gentle as she turned me around. She let out a low whistle. "This could've been a lot worse."

I was surprised at her lack of squeamishness. "I think his aim was crap."

"Well, y'know what they say, nobody

survives this long without at least a bit of luck here and there." She sounded like she spoke from experience.

Maybe I would have to do some digging on her.

Kennedy gently felt around the knife wound. "I think I could stitch this up for you. Thanks to your shoulder blade, it didn't go in too deep. But you should get it x-rayed tomorrow to make sure it didn't nick the bone. The last thing you need is a bone shard piercing an artery or causing internal damage."

"What can I say?" I said on a heavy sigh. "The universe likes me."

Kennedy gave me a fond but exasperated look and took me by the elbow, steering me into the bathroom. After all this time in the dark, the bright fluorescent lighting had me blinking and squinting.

Kennedy had me sit down on the edge of the bathtub, facing away from it, while she stood in the tub itself. "You have supplies?"

"Behind the bag of extra toilet paper." I winced as I shifted and felt the knife in me again. "And there's plenty of alcohol in the kitchen."

"Nice try. There's plenty in this kit to clean the wound without it."

She's really got my number, huh, I thought to myself.

Kennedy had never tried to keep me in line before. I'd appreciate that. Between my brother and my father, and then women who wanted me to be someone I wasn't, or clearly wanted to keep a hold of me and make me their official boyfriend... I wasn't exactly keen on the idea of someone else trying to order me around.

But I didn't mind Kennedy bossing me. Just a little. Especially not when it was so that she could patch me up and help keep me alive. I could see the lines of worry around her eyes and the corners of her mouth, even if she kept her tone light and calm.

For some reason, the idea that she was trying to hide her worry from me meant more than if she'd been wringing her hands and crying over me. Probably because she was aware I dealt with this on a regular basis and had gone through worse—if I didn't make a big deal out of it, neither would she.

Kennedy got the supplies all set out. "How attached are you to this shirt?"

"Not very, but I've got a fondness for the jacket." Good leather jackets weren't exactly off the rack.

"All right. I'll pull the knife out, and you'll take off the jacket. We'll cut the shirt open, and then I'll stitch up the wound. Fair?"

"Fair." It would be easier to just get the jacket off than try to cut through it, anyway.

I felt Kennedy's palm on my back, bracing. "On the count of three, I'm going to pull it out, okay?"

"Okay."

"One—"

I swore in pain as she neatly pulled the knife out in one smooth, powerful motion. I glared at her as Kennedy set the knife down in the sink.

She shrugged, completely unapologetic. "You would've tensed up at three."

…fair enough.

I shrugged quickly out of the jacket. Now that the knife was gone, my wound was going to bleed, badly. It was why I hadn't tried to remove the knife earlier. I knew of a lot of guys who'd had wounds that were treatable but they'd tried to get the knife or bullet or what-have-you out too soon and they'd bled to death.

Once the jacket was off, I sat back down on the tub. Kennedy pressed her hand to the knife wound and I held in a hiss of pain. It was good, both for her to brace and so the bleeding was somewhat held in while she efficiently cut open the back of the shirt.

I could feel the way the fabric had become thick with blood as she peeled it away from my shoulder. I heard Kennedy sigh, and then she ran the tub for a second. I realized why when I felt a warm, wet cloth wiping at my shoulder—cleaning the blood so she could get a good look at the wound.

"Where'd you learn to do this?" I asked.

"My dad was in construction and was kind of the neighborhood handyman. He taught me everything he knew, I was his little assistant." I could hear the smile in Kennedy's voice—and the wistfulness. "It's inevitable that you get injured at some point, and it's better to be prepared for the worst. So he taught me a lot of stuff. Then after he died and my mom got sick… I just got used to taking care of people, I guess."

I winced but held still as she cleaned and disinfected, then winced again as she slid the needle through my flesh.

"Will you get this x-rayed tomorrow?" she asked, like she knew I'd avoid it otherwise.

"Yes." I resisted the urge to tease her about it. *I just got used to taking care of people.*

This meant something to Kennedy. Did that mean that I meant something to her? Did I want to mean something to her?

Did she mean something to me?

There was silence for a few minutes, and then Kennedy said quietly, "I know that you don't talk about your work a lot. But… what were you doing? You've never come home injured before."

"That you know of."

"I'd know," Kennedy said, and there was such conviction in her voice that I suddenly wondered if she'd really been asleep all those times before or if she'd just been pretending, making sure I was okay and then minding her own business.

That oddly comforted me. She was giving me space but also looking out for me.

"I'm not sure what I'm doing, and that's the problem," I admitted.

I grimaced and grunted as she continued with her stitches. I was going to need to get a tattoo to cover this scar up. Some guys thought a lot of scars made them look tough, but I preferred to look invincible. Like I'd never had a scratch on me.

"I'm a soldier," I said quietly. "Do you know what that means?"

"You fight?" Kennedy hazarded a guess.

"Kind of. I mean, yes, I fight. But I'm a grunt. I do whatever bodyguard or overseeing work needs to be done. If a guy is trouble, I eliminate him."

"Leave him sleeping with the fishes?" Kennedy joked.

"Basically." I wished it was as bloodless as that. "I'm still trusted but I'm not an organizer, I'm not one of the lieutenants, so to speak. I like it that way. But lately my brother's been sending me on assignments that don't make any damn sense."

"...Vincent?" Kennedy asked, guessing at which brother I meant.

"Yeah, Vincent. Dante's the baby and a lawyer. Thinks he's above all of us."

Kennedy didn't offer any words of sympathy, which I appreciated. They would've rung hollow, anyway.

"I'm not sure what Vincent wants, but he's having me deliver packages all over the place. Different sizes but all on the smaller end, and usually at the dead of night. Then tonight I pick one up, and I get jumped. I got away, obviously, but these were real professionals. No accents but I'm pretty sure they're Russian. And I delivered the package to a Chinese restaurant of all fucking places. So I want to know what I'm risking my damn life for."

"I thought in the mafia you were always risking your life," Kennedy pointed out.

"Look, I'd die for my family, okay? Including Dante. They're my blood. You don't go against family no matter what and I love 'em even if sometimes I can't stand 'em." I felt her tie off the end of the stitches and I turned to look her in the eye. "But this is different. I want to know what I'm risking my life *for*."

Kennedy made me turn around again so she could finish cleaning up. "Sounds like you want your brother to trust you and you're afraid he doesn't."

"This feels like a test," I admitted, rubbing my fingers across my weary brow.

"Finished," Kennedy said quietly. Then I felt her lips press right below the closed-up wound, a brush of warmth and affection before she pulled away.

My heart clenched and I had to swallow a few times. I stood up, then examined myself in the mirror. "Nice work."

"Thanks." Kennedy cleaned everything up. "I think you should ask your brother what he's up to. And without yelling," she added.

I glanced at her. "Are you serious?"

She shrugged. "You were attacked. This is dangerous. You deserve to know what he's planning. And let's be honest here if your brother were to have a heart attack or something, you're the heir. Wouldn't you need to know his plans? Especially if those plans got him killed?"

"You know," I said, bracing a hand on the sink, "you think like a *mafioso*."

"I'll take that as a compliment," Kennedy replied ruefully.

"Good, it was meant as one." I watched her as she put everything away. "Would you like to go to my brother's wedding with me?"

Kennedy nearly dropped the kit. "I —what?"

"Vincent's getting married. I've been told to bring a plus one." I tactfully didn't mention that I'd been requested not to bring a stripper. "What do you say?"

"You really want me there?" Kennedy finished putting the kit away and stood up. "You want me to... meet your family?"

"Why wouldn't I? You're more than your profession, even if some people still think it's something to sneer at."

Kennedy bit her lip. "I just know how... close mafia are. I don't want to... intrude."

"You wouldn't be. You'd be my honored date. Nobody would bother you." I'd bust their heads open if they tried it. "It'll be fun.

And you can meet the people I've been complaining so much about to you."

Kennedy cracked a smile at that. "Well, if you're sure."

"I'm sure."

"Then all right. I would like to meet your family." She paused. "Only if you take some medication and *not* alcohol and get an x-ray tomorrow."

I snorted. This woman was going to get crazy ideas if I let her boss me around about this.

I let her boss me around about it anyway.

CHAPTER 12

Kennedy

Marco had invited me to his family's wedding.

Holy shit.

This was big. This was *good* big. This meant he trusted me, and that he liked me enough to want to show me to his family. I told Johnson right away the next day after Marco had gone to get his x-ray done.

He agreed with me that this was good news, and also that I shouldn't wear a wire.

There was no guarantee that business would be talked about and the risk was just too great. But if I could keep my eyes and ears open, the information I gathered at this shindig could help other undercover officers and tactical teams in planning their next move not just on the Russo family but on any other families who attended the wedding.

More than that—it was proof that Marco trusted me. It meant I could ask him questions without him wondering why. I could finally start to gather some real information.

Like this package business. What was it about? Why had it nearly gotten him killed, and why wasn't Vincent telling him about its significance? I could still see the blood on my hands when I closed my eyes—Marco's blood. It had scared me, even if I'd struggled not to show it. I knew that Marco was tough, that he would be fine, but I suddenly remembered all over again how fragile our bodies were. How just one small accident, hitting your head wrong, tripping, a knife two inches to the right, could suddenly end your life.

Thankfully he'd bought my story about my dad. My dad *was* in construction, and I had learned how to fix up homes and stuff from him, along with some basic first aid knowledge. But stitching up a wound? That level of battlefield medicine had come from my FBI training.

Not that I'd expected to use it on anyone other than myself in this mission.

I'd been unable to resist pressing a kiss to the stitches. I didn't know why. It had just felt… right. Like I had to give it a benediction somehow, some kind of good luck charm.

That part I didn't tell Johnson. Not just the wound but the package deal, too. I reasoned with myself that it would be foolish to tell him when I didn't even know what was going on myself with the situation. Moving packages around? That was weird and definitely meant something, but until I knew what that something was, why tell my superior about it?

Ah, yes, sir, they're doing something weird, but we don't know why or what it means! I'll be sure to keep you posted.

No, it would be best, or so I told myself, to wait until I had something substantial.

Of course, there was also the voice in the back of my head that told me the reason I hadn't told Johnson wasn't about professionalism. It was because I wanted to protect Marco.

But that was a ridiculous thought, so I ignored it.

Instead I busied myself making the bed, heading back to my apartment to keep everything in order, and just trying not to think about Marco talking to his brother, and that information, and what sort of choices I would have to make and what kind of game I'd have to play now that he had brought me so intimately into his life.

I'd been extremely successful in faking reluctance to go to the wedding. As I'd hoped, it just made him insist, and convinced him I was a person uninterested in his wealth or power. I'd have to keep playing that game if I wanted to succeed in getting information out of him the way that I had last night.

Oh, and I needed to buy a dress for the wedding.

Marco would probably offer to pay for me to get something, but I had enough money from stripping that I could certainly pay for a nice dress for myself. Nothing too extravagant. This was going to be a summer wedding, so I went out and did a little shopping.

It was odd, when the saleswomen would ask me what I was looking for. "I'm going to meet my boyfriend's family," I would tell them. "It's for his brother's wedding."

It sounded so normal. The saleswomen would always coo and give me advice on how to impress the parents, and I didn't know how to handle this... strange normalcy. After all, their usual advice wasn't going to help when the family of your boyfriend were in the mafia. And it would help even less if you were also an FBI agent undercover and faking everything to get information.

Was I faking everything? I no longer knew.

After shopping at a few different places, I found the dress I wanted, a summery, bright yellow number that had short cap sleeves and a skirt that stopped right at my knees. Fun and cute but not too revealing. I was sure that Marco wouldn't go out of his way to tell anyone my profession but I wanted to avoid looking like a stripper in general anyway.

Not that his family wouldn't assume that's what I was. Johnson had said in my original file briefing that Marco had a habit of bringing strippers and other women that his father deemed 'unsuitable' to family gatherings just to piss the old man off.

Was that what I was? But no, Marco hadn't asked it like he wanted to use me to annoy his family. He said it like he wanted to really show me off. Like he was proud of me and our relationship.

Warmth rose up in me at the thought and I tamped it down, purchasing the dress. I'd show this to Marco, get his approval, and then I'd go home and get ready for work. Simple as that. No warm fuzzy feelings to confuse me and ruin my day.

I got to his apartment and was shown to the private elevator by the doorman, but once I got up there, I could hear arguing.

Uh-oh.

The elevator dinged open, causing a pause in the conversation. Since the elevator opened right onto the penthouse apartment, there was no way for either man to avoid knowing I was there. Just turning around and heading back down while pretending I hadn't heard anything was not an option.

Marco stood in the middle of the room, wearing a t-shirt and jeans, barefoot. Across from him, in an impeccably tailored suit, was another man who I recognized from photos to be none other than Vincent Russo, the oldest brother.

The two of them looked very similar—same hair, same eyes, same height—but the way they held themselves was as different as night and day. Vincent looked like he had just come from a board meeting and was none too pleased to be interrupted, while Marco looked like he was about to start a fight in a dive bar.

Both men stared at me as I entered. I cleared my throat. How the hell were you supposed to behave when interrupting an argument between your sort-of boyfriend and his brother, who you'd also never met before?

"Hi." I stuck out my hand. "I'm Kennedy, I'm Marco's girlfriend. You must be Vincent."

I didn't want to simper, since I was sure Vincent would take that for fakeness, and if Marco had told me anything about him, he would know that those things hadn't been pleasant. So I kept my tone polite but professional and my face soft but unsmiling.

Vincent shook my hand. He had a firm handshake, and I could feel the power in his fingers. He could probably kill me barehanded.

"His girlfriend." Vincent looked over at Marco. "Have you told *him* that?"

"Don't be a dick," Marco snapped. "We've been together a month and she's my plus one to your own damn wedding."

"You can't hold it against me if I'm a little skeptical." Vincent turned to look at me once more. His gaze was assessing and sharp. "An actual girlfriend? For our Marco? Father will be pleased. What do you do?"

"I work in construction," I said, the lie

sliding easily off my tongue. Odd how it was easier to lie for Marco's sake rather than to deceive him. "Family business. But I'm sort of between jobs at the moment. I was taking care of my mother during her illness and she recently passed."

"My condolences for your loss," Vincent said, his tone perfectly gracious.

Marco scowled at him. "What."

"Oh it's nothing," Vincent said. "It's just I think I recall seeing a stripper that looks very much like your Kennedy here, the last time I was at Cozy Bunny."

"You mean when your future wife nearly got herself murdered?" Marco snapped back.

Vincent's eyes blazed. "Careful how you talk about my fiancée."

"Then you be careful how you talk about *my* girl."

"Touché," I pointed out.

Vincent looked over at me and I shrugged. "What, only the man's allowed to stand up for his partner now?"

That seemed to throw him. Vincent blinked. Marco grinned proudly.

"A month, you said?" Vincent asked his brother. "Well. That's good. Must be an extraordinary woman to get you to settle down for even that long."

"Great, maybe it also shows you I'm settled enough to hear what you're planning."

Oh, so this was what the argument was about.

"It's a need-to-know basis," Vincent said. "And you don't need to know."

"I don't need to know?" Marco repeated incredulously. "I was stabbed and nearly jumped by two assassins just to deliver a package to a Chinese restaurant! And a cheap purse shop! And a tailor's!"

Wait.

My mind raced, thinking back to other open operations I knew going on at the bureau. Why hadn't the restaurant tipped me off before? The Chinese mafia were the biggest movers of counterfeit luxury items in the city, specifically fashion items like purses, watches, and sunglasses. Marco had guessed that the men who'd tried to jump him were Russian, and the Russians were the main players in the mob world nowadays, with the Italians like the Russo family running a close second.

The packages were all small, being delivered in the early hours, and what you would call a 'single shipment'—not a big collection of packages or goods, just one offs.

Hmm.

I folded my arms. "You're trying some kind of deal with the Chinese," I said.

Vincent whipped around to stare at me. "And how would you know something like that?"

I shrugged. "All right, you got me, I'm a stripper at Cozy Bunny. But I wasn't lying about my mother. Point is, we hear a lot at that club, all you bigwigs talking to each other like we're not even there. And even more than that, we often benefit from the Chinese. I can't tell you how many of my coworkers are given knockoffs by their boyfriends who try to pass it off as no, really honey, it's a genuine Louis Vuitton! I promise!" I imitated the heavy Brooklyn accent of a lot of the mobsters, then rolled my eyes.

Marco snorted with laughter. Vincent didn't take his eyes off me. I tried to keep my attitude light. If Vincent suspected that there were other reasons why I knew so much, he'd probably be able to find out my true identity. Not that I thought the FBI did a lazy job of protecting its undercover workers but because Vincent Russo was supposedly that good. And I didn't doubt he actually was.

"Marco said that the guys who jumped him were probably Russian. Everyone knows the Russians are your biggest rivals. You don't have to be working at the strip club long to know that much. So you're trying to set something up with the Chinese."

"Something along those lines, yes," Vincent said carefully. "I knew strippers were a lot smarter than people liked to claim but you're something else, Miss Kennedy."

I had a feeling he'd be looking into me. I just had to hope that whatever this plan was, and his own wedding, would be enough to distract him for the time being. If all went well, by the time Vincent Russo figured out who I really was I'd be gone, back to my old life, and preparing to clap him in irons along with the rest of his family.

"You couldn't let me in on any of this?" Marco demanded.

"This isn't something to talk about in front of… non-family," Vincent said.

"Screw you. Kennedy's been more family to me than you and Dad have been for a while. If you trusted me at all you would've told me what you were planning."

"And risk it getting out? Everyone knows you talk too much in bed, Marco. I trusted you to deliver these packages, that should say plenty already about my faith in you."

"Did you think I was too dumb?" Marco snapped. "Too dumb to understand how to keep my mouth shut, or to understand what game you were playing?"

I quickly stepped in between, my hands up. "Okay, I think tempers are getting a little heated and I'm not sure that anything productive is going to be said. Vincent… I'd like to ask you to leave. Let's all calm down, take some time, and come back to this tomorrow, all right?"

Vincent stared me down. I stared right

back. I tried not to look like I was angry or challenging him, just calm. Like he couldn't ruffle me.

My heart beat wildly in my throat. You didn't really get to stand up to Vincent Russo and walk away in one piece, or at least, that's what everyone said.

Finally, Vincent looked away from me, to Marco. "We'll finish this conversation later."

He turned and walked out, the elevator doors sliding silently shut behind him.

I looked over at Marco, who ran a hand through his hair. "I'm going to take a shower."

For a moment I was confused. Take a shower? After that? Why?

Then I looked at his eyes and saw how red-rimmed they were, thought about how tight his voice had sounded. And I thought about how much pride a Russo man must have.

I waited until I'd heard the shower running for a little while and then I entered the bathroom, stripping down and slipping into the shower.

Marco was facing away from me. I saw

his shoulders stiffen, knew that he knew I was there, but he didn't turn around.

I wrapped my arms around him from behind and rested my cheek between his shoulder blades. I could see his injury, a bit pink from perhaps rubbing or whatever had been done at the doctor's office, but otherwise looking the same as it had last night, the stitches intact.

I had no idea how long we stood there like that, with me holding him. I was painfully aware that this could've been the wrong move—that he could have ordered me out, *kicked* me out, for invading during such a private and vulnerable moment.

But he didn't. He just let me hold him until he was finished.

Marco turned around. I didn't say a word, I just took his face in my hands and kissed him.

Something in him relaxed, I could feel it, and his hands settled gently at my waist to kiss me back. This wasn't a prelude to anything. I wasn't going to initiate sex, and I didn't think Marco was, either. It was just... kissing. Sweet and affirming.

I couldn't remember the last time I'd kissed someone just for the sake of it.

We rested our foreheads together. "Thank you," he said at last. His voice was soft.

"It's what I'm here for," I told him, and the words burned my tongue. Partially because they weren't true. Partially because they didn't feel like a lie.

CHAPTER 13

Marco

I didn't wait around for Vincent to come back to my apartment. The next morning while Kennedy was still asleep, resting after her shift the night before, I went to Vincent's office.

Vincent had his own lovely little apartment, but I wasn't going to go there. Partially to show him that I could be more courteous than he was, partially because he would probably be in his office at this time of the morning, and partially because Marla

Preston looked like she was very much the type to murder a man for disturbing her sleep.

Okay, so I was a little scared of my future sister-in-law. Sue me.

Vincent was indeed at his office, as was Toby, apparently going over the accounting books. Good luck to any poor idiotic sap who tried to skive and make a bit of money on the side in the Russo family. Vincent would find out so fast he'd have you in the Hudson with cement shoes before you even had the chance to say 'mea culpa'.

He looked up as I entered and Toby wisely beat a hasty retreat. "I'm kind of in the middle of something."

"You're always in the middle of something. Especially with the wedding. How many cake tastings are you going to today?"

Vincent looked up at the ceiling like he was asking God for patience. "Marco…"

I straightened my shoulders. "You want me to be serious."

"If it wouldn't be too much trouble."

My brother's lack of faith in me hurt. It hurt a whole fucking lot. I was willing to take a knife or anything else for him but he couldn't even give me the courtesy of warning me there might be a knife coming?

Normally I would've kicked whatever woman was with me out of the apartment so I could have my privacy. I wasn't about to let just anyone see me like that. But Kennedy wasn't just anyone. She'd been different from the start, and she'd stuck up for me to my brother. She'd done it in a way that Vincent would respect, too, none of the yelling and lecturing that would've turned him right off. Instead she'd stayed calm, showed him how smart she was. Hadn't looked at all ruffled by a mafia *capo* in her space.

I'd been so damn proud of her in that moment. I knew I'd picked the right girl to finally give this relationship thing a shot with.

When I'd gone into the shower, I hadn't expected her to join me. Kennedy was good about giving me space. But instead she slipped in with me and just… held me. She hadn't tried to talk to me, or ask me how I was doing, or force me to address the disappointment and hurt that I felt.

She'd just been there. Supporting me. Her arms had been comfort enough, and I'd felt supported for the first time in years instead of just… constantly alone, looked down on by my father and ignored by my brothers.

I tried to hold onto that feeling as I faced Vincent now. "Look, I know that I haven't done a lot to prove to you that I'm responsible. But I've been trying to improve things. This thing with Kennedy? I want to try and make it last. I don't know what it is with her, but I want her around more than I've ever wanted any other woman. And I want you to trust me. But I can't prove to you that I'm trustworthy and responsible if you don't give me a chance.

"You say you trust me enough to have me be the one to run these packages because you know I'm the best but—I can't do my job well if I don't know what the hell I'm protecting or running. You gotta let me in on this or I'm gonna screw up because I don't know enough."

Vincent stood up and leaned forward on his desk. "I want to trust you, Marco, but this is dangerous. I'm playing a difficult game here."

"Screwing over the Russians? Kennedy hit the nail on the head there, didn't she? She's smart."

"Possibly too smart. Can you really trust her, Marco? Did you run a background check on her?"

"Jade runs a background check on all her girls, she's clean. Besides, you picked Marla Preston, you can't judge me on my choice."

"At least I picked a mafia girl. You don't know where this Kennedy could be from."

"But was she right?" I demanded. "Was she right about your plans?"

Vincent sighed. "Sort of. She was on the money for the information she had at her disposal and what she thinks is exactly what I want the Russians to think—that I'm striking a deal with the Chinese under the table through their fake-luxury-goods operation."

"What are you really doing?"

"Oh, just providing enough funds for the indentured people to buy a way out of their contract," Vincent said innocently. "All marked with the Petrov symbol, of course."

The way that many mafia gangs had operated over the years was to pay for a person to come to America, but then they had to work off the debt that they owed. It was miserable, and many never worked that debt off at all. It was indentured servitude. I called it slavery and I was damn glad that Dad didn't operate that way.

"So the Chinese think that the Petrov family is releasing all of their work force to cripple their operations through mass walkouts," I said. "And the Russians think that the Chinese are scheming behind their backs with… us?"

"Well, not with *us*…" Vincent smirked. "The Caruso family's been getting a little uppity. I had Toby leave a few breadcrumbs. The Russians know *someone's* fucking with the Chinese trying to undermine the Petrovs but they don't know who. If they're smart, they'll follow that trail and figure out it's the Carusos."

"And if they're not smart?"

"Not my problem, they can blame whoever they want. As long as the delivery guy isn't caught, we're in the clear. And you don't get caught."

No, I didn't. Ever.

"I needed someone who would make sure the package didn't fall into the hands of anyone who intercepted it, otherwise..." Vincent held up his hands. "Game over. They'd see what was really in the packages and know what stunt we were trying to pull. And I needed someone who wouldn't get caught themselves otherwise the Chinese would know what we were up to. Either way we'd be screwed. But I knew you'd come through."

"You trusted me enough to be a good soldier but not enough to actually know what the bigger plan was?" I shook my head. "That's not going to fly, Vincent. If anything were to happen to you, I'd have to step up and help Dad out. And I can't do that if I don't know anything."

Vincent shook his head right back at me. "I want to trust you but come on, Marco, when have you or Dante given me any reason to think you could handle the family business? You're an adrenaline junkie."

"Y'know, that's why I like Kennedy so much. She's the first person to know that's not all I am." I jabbed my finger onto the desk. "You and Dad have known me my entire life and you still think so fucking little of me. This woman's known me a month and she gives me more credit than you two ever did."

"You sure she's not just trying to get on your good side?"

"Kennedy could do a lot better than me, trust me. I had to practically beg her to commit to our relationship and you know I don't beg." I straightened. "Keep me in the fucking loop, Vincent, or don't include me at all. None of this in-between shit."

Vincent looked at me. "Will you be responsible and actually come to me with problems and play by the rules instead of complaining and cutting it fast and loose?"

We glared at each other. We were both stubborn sons of bitches when it came down to it—that trademark Russo refusal to back down. I had a lot of pride, and so did Vincent, and neither of us wanted to be the first one to break.

I saw his shoulders relax a little and I let out a breath, saying, "Fine," at almost the same moment that he did.

Vincent held out his hand for me to shake. I laughed. "What are we, fuckin' business partners?"

He rolled his eyes. "Suit yourself."

"By the way," I added, "Kennedy's my plus one to the wedding."

"She's *what*?"

CHAPTER 14

Kennedy

I was terrified of going to this wedding.

I was aware that was kind of silly of me. A wedding? A social gathering? That's what had me all tied up in knots? But in my defense, this was a mafia wedding. This wasn't just a group of family and friends who were invited —this was political. All of the Russo allies would be there, including some not-exactly-allies that the Russos couldn't afford to *not* invite if they wanted to keep the peace. One of those families was the Petrovs, the very ones that owned New York and were currently being fucked with by Vincent Russo.

Marco gave me a *very* appreciative once-over when he saw me in the dress I'd picked out. "Good choice."

He was in a suit, of course, since he'd be one of the groomsmen. Marco had said that he and Vincent patched things up, but he didn't tell me anything further, and I decided this wasn't something I could pry about. Maybe it would give me good information, maybe it wouldn't, but either way I had to be careful not to seem too curious about Marco's relationships. He and Vincent had come to some sort of agreement, and that was what mattered to me. Through Marco, I might be able to get more important information.

Of course, no matter how much or how little the brothers were fighting wouldn't matter. Marco and his youngest brother, Dante, would be groomsmen at the wedding to keep up appearances and stop gossip.

I hadn't told Johnson about the whole...

game that Vincent was playing with two other families. Playing them against each other, making them paranoid and angry. He was basically starting a war, and hoping the two would both be so weak he could use it to swoop in and claim some power and territory for himself.

This was big, especially with the D.A. planning something on their own end… and with our undercover operatives in the field. This would throw everyone off their game and cause chaos.

But I still hadn't said anything.

Why?

I told myself it was too early. If I shared this with my superiors and then word spread, Vincent Russo would know for sure who'd blabbed. I had to wait until a few more people knew about this. That way he couldn't trace any leaks back to me.

That wasn't the only reason, though. Even if I pretended that it was.

"Lookin' good, handsome," I teased Marco as he fiddled with his cufflinks and tie.

"I always hate these things. Vincent and Dante are the suit guys, not me."

"You could always show up in your motorcycle gear, kick the wedding off with a nice fashion scandal."

I stepped forward and did up his cuff-links, then his tie. The groomsmen were in soft dove grey suits, perfect for the weather and matching the lighter color theme that the bride had gone with. I thought it paired rather nicely with my bright yellow dress.

"Thanks." Marco watched me through dark eyes as I set him to rights, like he wasn't sure whether to be in awe of me or to ravish me.

I shivered. I wasn't quite sure what to do with Marco, either. The hot sex was one thing. But I'd seen a much more vulnerable and wounded side to him after his fight with his brother. Now… I didn't know what to do about that.

Well. I knew what I wanted. I wanted to protect him. But I couldn't do that. It was my job to do the opposite.

My heart and my head weren't in agreement and that disturbed me.

"Let's get this over with," Marco said, giving me his arm.

We weren't taking the motorcycle, partially to keep from ruining our clothes with creases and partially because Vincent had said if Marco showed up with it, Marco would be short a vital organ. Instead, we took a town car.

"I thought the bride was the one who made a big fuss over everything," I murmured as we got in.

"Honestly, Marla seems chill compared to Vincent, trust me," Marco muttered back. "And that's saying something."

I had never met Marla, the intended wife, before and I braced myself for some Type A control freak.

I also braced myself for… well, just about anything.

We got to the church and I was immediately separated from Marco as a wedding planner with dyed-blonde hair and a terrifyingly calm smile directed him to the back of the church where his brothers and other groomsmen gathered. She then turned her attention to me. "You must be the girlfriend."

"Yes ma'am." I felt suddenly like a meek schoolkid facing the principal.

The woman checked her clipboard. "You'll be at the front, left-hand side."

All the way at the front? That couldn't be right. I wasn't family, even if I was Marco's plus one. But I didn't dare argue with the woman—I think I'd rather tell Marco I worked undercover—and I did as I was told.

The front two pews on the left-hand side of the aisle were sparsely populated. I cast my mind back to my briefings. The man who'd started the Russo family had come from Florence, the second son tasked with building the empire in the new world. He'd had two sons, one who'd died and been erased from family history, and the one who now ran the family, Antonio. He had three sons, all accounted for at the altar.

That would explain why there was room for me at the front. Any extended family the Russos had would be back in Italy and while some might've made the trip (and had, judging by the few people in those rows) it wasn't enough to fill the place.

Marla Preston's side looked pretty empty, too. There were just her parents and then a couple people who looked like cousins or perhaps aunts.

The rows behind them, though, were steadily filling up on either side of the aisle. It was pretty easy to guess that everyone had been assigned seats in family groups and that families had been strategically placed so that nobody who hated each other had to sit close by. Not that I really thought anyone would start something in a church. If any bad blood was going to bubble up it would probably be at the reception.

I took a seat in the second-to-front row, worried that if I sat in the very front it would seem presumptuous. Marco stood with Vincent, a couple of men from other families, and another man who had to be Dante. He looked like someone had taken Vincent and softened the sharp edges, smoothed them out a little.

The eyes, though, were just as sharp as those of his brothers. Dante Russo was supposed to be the law-abiding citizen, the straight-shooter, but he didn't look like he was any less ambitious or calculating than the rest of his family. I'd have to be just as wary around him as I was around anyone else here.

A man sitting in the row in front of me turned around, and I nearly jumped out of my skin as I stared *Don* Russo full in the face.

He looked very much like his sons, but there was no warmth to him. I felt like the man had been carved out of a glacier.

"When Vincent told me that Marco was bringing someone, I knew it would be one of those ridiculous bimbos he loves to flaunt," the man said. His voice was quiet but sharp. "At least you've dressed yourself respectably."

My instinct was to lash out. I hadn't gotten through the FBI Academy because I'd been soft or let people walk all over me. Normally I'd give this old asshole a piece of my mind.

But I had to play it carefully here. I had to be smart.

Antonio Russo thought little of his son's maturity, but cared about him far more than he wanted to let on, a fact that Marco knew and tried to be understanding about. Maybe I could use that.

"Marco wanted me to be sure to dress

nicely," I replied, my voice soft but not shy. "He wants this day to go well for Vincent. He's been worried about it."

The head of the Russo family stared me down. I stared right back at him. I wasn't going to be disrespectful, but I would not be cowed.

"What's your name?" Antonio Russo asked. "And I mean your real one."

I couldn't be sure if this man actually knew things about me already because of Vincent, or if he was just making assumptions. "My name is Kennedy. You must be Mr. Russo. It's good to finally put a face to the name."

I wasn't about to lie and say it was a pleasure to meet him. I had a feeling that he would see right through me and would be annoyed.

"Complained about me a lot, has he?"

"No, actually. Marco cares a lot about you." Again, I couldn't lie and say Marco respected him, even if I suspected that was actually the case. Marco would probably rather die than admit that. "So he only complains about you sometimes. Once a week."

The head of the Russo crime family stared at me, and then chuckled quietly. Even his chuckle was cold. No wonder these boys had turned into the kind of men they had. I wondered about Mr. Russo's wife, Marco's mother, and what kind of woman she must have been to warm up this glacier.

"You seem more on your toes than the last dozen," Mr. Russo finally stated.

"Life's given me a lot to stay on my toes about," I replied. "You can worry about plenty of things at the reception, Mr. Russo. I believe the chief concern should be keeping the Petrovs in line. But I won't be one of those things."

Mr. Russo peered at me. His gaze was one of the most piercing I'd ever met. It was hard not to squirm. I felt like he could see right through me, like I had an FBI badge stamped on my heart and he'd be able to find it.

"See that you aren't," he said eventually, and then he turned around to face front again.

I slowly, silently let out a breath of relief. I

hadn't expected approval, but it wasn't condemnation. I'd take it.

Everyone settled, Vincent took his spot, and the bridesmaids walked down the aisle. A couple of them seemed to be Marla's friends or family, since they looked genuinely happy to be there. A couple others looked blank—probably hiding sourness—and I remembered the shockwaves that had rippled through the mafia world (and our division) when Vincent Russo had chosen to marry this random woman and not some powerful don's daughter.

Some of those daughters were probably still sore over it.

Then the music changed and Marla walked in.

She didn't look at all how I'd pictured her. There was something both demure and coy about her. She carried herself like a queen, but a benevolent one. And the way she looked at Vincent made me not only reconsider how I should view him, it made me…

I tore my gaze away from Marla and looked over at Vincent. He stared back at her like she was the only person in the room, a look of pure adoration on his face. I'd never seen him look like that before. Hell, I hadn't thought Vincent Russo *could* look like that.

I want Marco to look at me like that.

Envious. Marla and Vincent made me *envious.*

Now that I'd had the thought, I couldn't take it back. I couldn't unknow it. I wanted Marco to look at me with that same level of love and adoration on his face. I wanted to be able to look at him the way Marla looked at Vincent, openly and unashamedly in love.

But I couldn't ever have that. I was going to put Marco and the rest of his family, including this lovely couple, in prison. Marla and Vincent would be separated. And I'd never get to be with Marco again. Even if he wanted me, for some insane reason—it was hard to have a proper relationship when one of you were in jail. Given the number of enemies the Russos had, I didn't have high hopes for any of them living long in prison anyway.

As the vows were said and we all stood up to politely clap, my head swam. I felt like I was underwater with everything muffled. For the first time I was facing the truth that I'd worked so hard to skirt around: *I didn't want to turn Marco in.*

As if I'd summoned him, Marco appeared next to me, his arm wrapping around my waist. "Vincent and Marla are doing a receiving line but he wants us to go ahead to the reception and make sure everything's under control." He rolled his eyes. "I think he just wants to avoid me running into any exes in the crowd."

"How many do you have?" I asked lightly, completely unbothered by the prospect.

It didn't matter that Marco had exes among the mafia nobility. He hadn't dated them for as long as he'd dated me, and I was sure that he hadn't dared be as vulnerable and open to them because they'd just take it back to their families and use it.

Just like you're doing with the FBI.

I banished that thought, even as my stomach twisted uncomfortably.

Marco made a face. "Too many," he growled. "But to be fair, they were using me just like I was using them. It was all a game. Either they wanted to use me as a stepladder to get to my older brother, the actual heir—or they hoped to marry me and goad me into having some damn ambition and replacing my brother. None of which was going to happen so I just untangled myself from that nonsense as fast as I could."

"They should know that you'd never replace Vincent."

Marco looked at me with an odd light in his eyes, one that took me a minute to realize was appreciation. "Yes. Thank you."

"A girl's gotta appreciate her man."

"And a man's gotta appreciate his girl. Too bad we don't have time to slip away and have a little fun."

"I'm trying to play nice with your family, get on their good side. A little afternoon delight is *not* going to help."

Marco laughed. "Fair. Let's go make sure the ice sculpture isn't melting or whatever."

My heart beat frantically in my chest as I followed him. *I want you to love me. I want you to love me. I want you to love me.*

I want to be allowed to love you.

CHAPTER 15

Marco

Kennedy looked stunning in her dress, the color showing off her skin and the length showing off her legs. I could feel her sticking close to me, probably unsure what to do to navigate this sea of sharks without getting bitten, but none of that nervousness ever showed to the people she spoke with. To the curious—and gossiping—people who came up to meet her, she was nothing but light laughs and calm smiles.

I introduced her to Marla once the happy couple arrived. Marla, I had to admit, was just as smart and tough as Vincent. I hadn't spent a lot of time with her—two deaths in the family were no joke—but now she seemed like she was finally ready to move on from her grief.

She smiled at Kennedy, asked about her family, expressed sympathy over the lingering illness and death of Kennedy's mother—the consummate hostess.

Dear old Dad watched it all like a hawk, of course. I wished there was some way to protect Kennedy from his gaze. One slip up and Dad would be after the both of us, which Kennedy frankly didn't fucking deserve.

I knew it was my own damn fault. I'd spoiled any good will or trust from previous big social gatherings thanks to my habit of bringing escorts and strippers or the dumbest heiress I could find. Instagram influencers, the daughters of celebrities, if they were beautiful, spoiled, and dumb, they'd fit my plan to outrage my father.

Now I had a woman that I actually really liked, that I wanted my dad to approve of, and he was understandably suspicious. Any ill-will directed at Kennedy was really my fault.

Which made me want to protect her even more.

"Marla and Kennedy seem to have really hit it off," I noted to Vincent as I watched the two women converse.

Kennedy seemed pleasantly surprised by Marla's personality, and I could tell the smile on her face right now was genuine.

"Mm." Vincent looked at me. "You genuinely have feelings for her."

"I wouldn't have put it like *that*," I grumbled.

Okay, so maybe I had some 'feelings' for Kennedy. If you wanted to frame it that way. "Why, is that a problem?" I challenged.

Vincent turned to face me. "Marco, please. I'm just trying to help. You know we have to be careful who we let in."

"You want to look into her." My voice was flat.

"I looked into Marla. It's how it goes."

I knew that. Of course I fucking knew that. This wasn't a hill that I could really afford to try and die on. But that didn't mean I had to be fucking happy about it. "I'll—"

Vincent held up a hand. "I'll look into her. You're compromised."

"Because I have *feelings* for her?" I did air quotes.

"Yes, Marco, for fuck's sake." Vincent rolled his eyes.

He looked like he might say something else, too, but then his gaze slid from me to over my shoulder. I turned around to see what the hell he was looking at, and saw that one of the Russians—I had no fucking clue which one—had somehow sidled up to Kennedy while I was distracted with my brother.

The guy had that stupid slicked-back hair look going on that always made someone look like they'd stepped out of a bad '80s movie about politicians. He had a look in his eyes that I didn't like in the least, and—his hand landed on Kennedy's upper arm.

Kennedy did an admirable job of pretending to laugh at whatever his stupid joke was, even as I saw fire blazing to life in her eyes.

I knew that Kennedy could take care of herself. Strippers generally did, since you never knew when a bouncer might be distracted and you'd have to take care of a bad customer yourself in the meantime. And nobody had a fire like my girl.

But in that split-second, it wasn't about whether or not Kennedy could defend herself. It was about some upstart prick trying to start a fight by thinking he could just put his hands on *my* girl.

Maybe he thought she was just another fling of mine and so it wouldn't matter to me. But even my flings were off limits. Once we'd parted ways? Have at 'em. But while they came back to my bed at night? They were *mine.*

It was even worse when it was the girl I loved.

The revelation didn't hit me as hard as it should have, because I was a little busy seeing red. I strode over, Vincent's quiet warning drowned out by the roaring in my ears.

"Watch where you're putting your hands," I snarled, grabbing the guy's wrist.

"Oh, what, can't handle your girl talking

to another man?" the guy snapped back at me. "We were just having a friendly conversation."

His smirk made me want to do something drastic. "How about you and my fist have a friendly conversation?" I shot back.

The guy cocked his eyebrow at me, daring me to do it.

Oh, I was more than happy to oblige him.

Maybe I wasn't a planner like my brother, or a fancy ass lawyer, but I sure as hell could throw a punch, and I knew which way the guy would dodge going by the way he shifted his weight. Always watch the hips—the hips'll show where the person planned to head next.

I swung hard, expecting the guy's dodge backwards, then tucked my arm back at the last minute and swung with my other arm. He was completely caught off-guard, stupid bastard, and when I sent my fist into his jaw he went down like a sack of fucking bricks, out cold.

Everyone stared at me.

Oh, shit.

"Marco!" My father's voice could've cut

through steel. "What exactly do you think you're doing?"

I straightened out my suit. "Just maintaining law and order, Father," I said.

Not even I would dare call my father 'Dad' or some variation in public.

My father was not amused. He turned to one of the men standing by—this one I recognized. He was a Petrov. I didn't know which one. It wasn't my job to keep all of them straight, that was Vincent's fun role. No, my job was just to recognize faces so that I would know if I was in trouble.

This guy, pretty sure he went by 'Alex' since most of 'em did just to fuck with the rest of us, was one of the Petrov lieutenants. Of course the old man who owned it all couldn't be bothered to come to the wedding himself, so he sent a couple of his higher-ranking guys so that we wouldn't be too offended to use the excuse to attack.

"My apologies," my father said, while I ground my teeth. "Such behavior will, of course, be dealt with."

To my surprise, I felt Marla step up beside me. "Marco didn't start it," she said.

I had to keep myself from gaping at her. Standing up to the Petrovs *and* my father? All right, so maybe Marla was a good match for my brother after all. She had a spine of steel, I could say that much.

"This *soldato* of course," Marla said, gesturing at the unconscious man on the ground, "was making unwanted advances towards my friend. Marco stepped in to defend her. He was goaded into it."

Both my father and the lieutenant started talking ferociously at the same moment, obviously both berating Marla, but Marla simply hissed back at the lieutenant in Russian. Whatever she said, it made the guy pale a little. I hoped she'd just told him she'd cut off his balls.

"Now." Marla smoothed her hands over the skirt of her wedding dress. "Perhaps we can dispense with any more unpleasantness at my wedding."

There was a hint of a threat in there and I was again impressed.

There were murmured apologies, although judging by the glare my father shot me, I wasn't going to be off the hook for long.

The moment this wedding reception was over I'd have my feet to the fire for my behavior.

"Men." Marla's lips quirked upwards into a small, amused smile. "The moment you get all angry because of some feminine thing they back off like you're practicing witchcraft."

"Thank you," I told her honestly. "Welcome to the family."

"The Petrovs are just sore that my Vince didn't choose one of them."

I grinned at her, then turned to see how Kennedy took this whole thing. She'd probably tell me that she'd been able to handle herself just fine, thanks, and I'd retort that didn't mean I was going to really leave her in the lurch.

After all, I'd brought her here. It was only fair that I keep the circling wolves at bay. What kind of guy would I paint myself as if I just left her to fend for herself? Everyone would know that I didn't really care about her. It wasn't about her ability to defend herself, it was about my willingness to stick up for her.

Not that anything in the damn world could've stopped me from sticking up for her. I was quickly realizing, with Kennedy, that I was a real jealous bastard.

But when I turned around, prepared for a verbal ass-kicking from my girl… she wasn't there.

I looked around. She wasn't anywhere.

"Kennedy?" I called out quietly, trying not to shout and draw attention to myself again.

Marla's eyebrows shot up. "She didn't strike me as the type to cut and run."

"She's not." I walked over to Vincent. "Did you see where Kennedy went? She's gone."

Vincent, to my surprise and gratitude, didn't make a retort. Instead he nodded at the ever-present Toby, who spoke quietly into an earpiece. After a moment, Toby shook his head. "Nobody in security's got eyes on her."

"She can't just have disappeared into thin air," I snapped. Something told me this was wrong. This was off. I was a soldier, I was in the battlefields every day, and I'd honed my instincts into a sharp, fine weapon. I had to listen to them and trust them or I would've been dead ten times over by now.

And right now, those instincts told me this was *bad*.

"Someone had to have seen something," Toby said. He didn't sound upset, but then, Toby never sounded upset. We could be in the middle of a nuclear apocalypse and Toby would sound perfectly fucking calm.

"We're all keeping a lookout," Vincent agreed. "Someone would've—"

I saw the light come on in his eyes right as I had the same exact thought. We looked at each other.

Someone would've seen something—unless they were all distracted by a fight.

Shit.

CHAPTER 16

Kennedy

A hand was clamped over my mouth the moment that Marco hit the guy.

I had to admit, it was a bold plan but an effective one. Something that they'd taught us in the academy was that it was better to move with confidence out in the open than to try and be sneaky about it. People could sense when you were nervous, or trying to slip something past them. The best thing to do was to act like you were given permission for whatever you were doing.

That was how con artists got into places all the time. Just stride up to a place with a clipboard and nobody asked questions. Pick up a headset, look like you were late to something, and no one would look twice.

And whoever had planned this knew what they were doing. The guy who'd been flirting with me… I wasn't sure what his name was or if he'd ever even given it to me… he had been just the right amount of annoying and flirty without taking it too far and setting *me* off before Marco got to him.

I'd seriously been weighing how much it would cost me if I told him to fuck off, though. I didn't want to make trouble for Marco and I was sure that whatever outburst I made would, somehow, be blamed on him by his father. So I'd tried to just politely get the guy to shove off.

Then he put his damn hand on my arm, squeezing slightly, and I'd seen Marla's eyebrows shoot up as she waited to see if I'd smack him. Actually I'd been planning to grab his wrist and dig my thumb into his pressure point, twisting his wrist and sending him to his knees—much more elegant and less attention-grabbing than a slap—but before I could do anything, Marco was there.

And then I was being grabbed.

I knew self-defense, of course, but the hand over my mouth wasn't bare. There was a small cloth held between the fingers, and the moment the smell hit me, I knew it was chloroform. Chloroform has a signature sickly sweet smell—and gave a wicked headache when you woke up.

Great. Just great.

The large garden where the reception was being held swam in front of me, and even though I tried not to breathe it in, it was too late—everything went fuzzy, tilted sideways, and was dark.

When I woke up, I had a moment of confusion—*where the hell was I, and why did my head hurt so much*—followed by a moment of inner panic.

Had Vincent or Mr. Russo himself found me out? Had I been dragged away so that they could interrogate me about what I had told to my superiors, and then they could dispose of me?

Slowly, inch by inch, I became more aware of my body. First my head, which was pounding. Then my wrists and ankles, which also hurt, and then the rest of my arms, my legs, slowly meeting in the middle until I could feel my torso, my neck, all of me.

I blinked and focused on breathing in and out. My neck had a crick in it and rested on something—something that allowed me to stare up at a high nondescript ceiling.

A chair. The back of a chair, that's what my neck rested on.

Slowly I lowered my head and my gaze. My head felt annoyingly heavy. The room swam into focus in front of me and I blinked a few times to clear my vision.

I was in the back room of… something. Somewhere. I wasn't sure. It was a bit cold, the kind that settled into the air and was so still that it somehow made it all worse. Everything was bare, but the kind of bare like recently it had been full of something and someone had just taken everything out of it to make it empty.

My feet shifted as I tested the ropes that bound me to this chair, and I felt the smooth thin plastic of tarp beneath my soles.

Shit.

It was basic practice to lay down tarp underneath your prisoner so that when you killed them, you could wrap up their body to dispose of it—and avoid leaving incriminating stains on the floor. Blood was notoriously difficult to get out of, well, just about any surface, which was why there were special companies who cleaned up crime scenes.

I looked around. There wasn't anyone in the room with me. I couldn't see any cameras, either, or listening devices, but that didn't mean they weren't in here.

Deep breaths, Kennedy, deep breaths.

I had to keep myself calm, at least on the inside. If I had to play the scared victim I would, but I couldn't *actually* be scared. I had to keep my wits about me and be ready for anything.

What if what you need to be ready for is death?

If this was Vincent's doing, or his father's,

I really didn't have a hope of getting out of here alive. They would've figured out who I was and if there was one thing that the mafia didn't tolerate, it was cops sneaking into their midst.

My pleas that I loved Marco, that I didn't want to betray him, wouldn't do me any good. First of all, why the hell would they believe me? Second of all, not wanting to do something didn't equal not doing that thing. And third of all, if Marco himself found out, he wouldn't want me anymore anyway so it was all a moot point. Of course Vincent would tell him. Vincent Russo would never keep such a secret from his brother, would he?

Maybe—maybe Vincent would kill me and blame it on someone else. The Petrovs, the Carusos, the Triad. It would make sense as a way to protect his brother's heart while also providing a neat excuse to further his own plans. I almost preferred that option. Better that Marco think I was loyal to him, and that he'd lost me, than for him to know that I was betraying him from the moment we met.

A door behind me opened, and I didn't bother twisting my head around to see who it was. I wasn't going to give them a performance of panic, or any other emotion, until I understood the situation better.

"Ah, good, she's awake." The voice wasn't Vincent's or that of his father. I didn't recognize the voice at all, in fact—except that there was a trace of a Russian accent.

Footsteps sounded as three men walked around to stand in front of me. Two of them I didn't recognize, but the one who'd spoken —I had seen him in various files at the bureau. He was Misha. Just full stop. Misha. No last name.

The Petrovs were so powerful partially because this was just the American branch. The real seat of power was still back in Russia, and while the old men in charge there tended to let their second sons here in the New World have a long leash, that didn't mean they weren't watched. Misha was one of the lieutenants sent over from Russia when one of the Petrov sons had proven himself a bit... queasy over doing what needed to be done in a mafia family.

Misha now handled most of the 'cleaning' jobs for the Petrovs. When Dmitri Preston had been murdered, we'd assumed Misha had been the one to take care of it, until we'd heard about how messy the murder was. The disappearance of Dmitri's brother, Alexander Preston, soon after? That was much more Misha's work. We had no idea what the Preston brothers had done to piss off the Petrovs, but clearly Vincent's working to undermine their relationship with the Chinese was now an act of retaliation. Even if he hadn't been marrying their sister, the Preston brothers were under the Russo family jurisdiction. To have dealt with them… that was a huge insult and violation of the many polite, unspoken mafia rules.

Now Misha had me. He couldn't touch Marla, obviously. The bride would be too heavily guarded. But Marco's new girl? The one girl he'd ever liked enough to keep around?

I made a prime kidnapping target.

Misha stared at me. I stared back, keeping my face blank. I didn't want to use up all my defiance at once, and Misha was not a man moved by tears or panic. And dammit, I had my pride. I was perfectly willing to play the part to some extent but not for a damn Russian mobster. I'd die with my pride and dignity as intact as possible.

Finally he looked at one of the other men. "All right, let's take the before pictures."

The before pictures. Jesus Christ.

"I'm ready for my close-up," I purred.

Misha chuckled. "I can see why the asshole likes you."

One of the goons came to stand behind me, either to help drive the point home in the pictures or just to manhandle me towards the camera if I got difficult. The other pulled out a camera and began taking pictures—with quite a lot of care, mumbling about lighting and everything.

Guess even mafia goons had hobbies.

"Tell me, Miss..." Misha snapped his fingers a few times, then waved his hand as if trying to recall my name.

"Kennedy."

"Ah, thank you. Very unusual and annoying name."

"My dad thought it was dignified."

Misha snorted. "Tell me, Miss Kennedy, do you know why you're here?"

"You hate the Russos?" I offered. I wasn't sure if I should play dumb, or share what I knew. One of those options would possibly keep me alive longer, but I didn't know which one.

Misha chuckled again. "Well of course. But is that all your boyfriend told you? And here I thought he was such a blabbermouth in bed."

"Marco's smarter than most of you seem to think," I said, unable to contain my loyalty.

"Just because the sex is good doesn't mean he's everything you want him to be," Misha said placidly. "Well, if you don't know, then I'll tell you. I'd hate for you to wonder why we're going to do the things to you that we… might very well have to do."

"I wasn't aware there was an option for you to *not* do those things," I pointed out.

"But of course!" Misha smiled. "That's the thing, Miss Kennedy. If I give your Marco the option—back off and I kill her kindly, keep pushing and I kill her slow—what kind of option is that? Either way you die, and I have to deal with the mess that follows. There should always be an option for you to live. Hope is the true curse—it incentivizes like nothing else."

Ah, we had a philosopher on our hands. Fantastic.

"So what *are* the options?" I asked.

Occasionally the camera would flash, blinding me for a split-second and disorienting me. I blinked the dancing bright spots out of my vision and tried not to let it annoy me.

Misha shrugged. "The options are that the Russos agree to back off in whatever... *scheme* it is they're up to—or you start to lose body parts. Every day they do not respond to our demands..." He eyed me. "You don't *really* need all your fingers, do you?"

My heart raced, but I breathed deeply and kept my face blank. I'd gone through training for this kind of thing and I wasn't going to let this man have the satisfaction of seeing me upset or scared. "You might as well kill me. The Russos will never give into any demands from another family. Even if Marco wanted to, he's not the one in charge. I'm nothing to

Don Russo, or Vincent, and they might love Marco but not enough to sacrifice their reputation for him."

I shrugged. "Besides, just because I've lasted longer than most doesn't mean I'm really all that special to him. He'll be out with another girl in a few days, just you watch."

Honestly, it hurt me to even say that. The idea of Marco forgetting about me so quickly and easily made me want to cry, or perhaps rage. I wanted to be as important to him as he was to me. I wanted him to love me, like I loved him.

Was he looking for me, right now? Was he wondering what had happened? I hoped so.

But then fear gripped me. What would happen if Marco got me back? I'd be right back where I started, working against him while wanting just to be with him. I'd still have to betray him.

A horrible sort of determination rose within me. I wondered if this was what it was like to be in the mafia, to have such loyalty to your family that you would rather face any kind of punishment rather than be known as a snitch.

"I think you're more special to him than you realize," Misha said enigmatically. He looked at his amateur photographer. "You finished?"

"*Da.*"

"Excellent. Let us get these to the Russos." He smiled at me. "Don't worry. I have a feeling you'll be safe and sound in your boyfriend's arms soon enough. Maybe even with most of your body intact."

I graced him, finally, with a show of my defiance. I smiled slow and wicked. "Or you're going to end up having to kill me. We'll soon find out who's right."

Whatever you do, Marco, I thought, *don't save me. Let me die.*

Let me die loyal.

CHAPTER 17

Marco

"Did you fucking see these?" I snarled, storming into Dad's office.

You did not storm into Dad's office. You did not storm into Dad's apartment. You did not 'storm' into anything that my father claimed as his. You waited to be summoned, or in extreme cases you made an appointment.

Good thing I thought rule-following was for the spineless.

I slammed the photographs down onto his desk, on top of some papers covered in numbers. "They've got her. The fucking *Petrovs* have Kennedy, all because you and Vincent decided to fucking meddle."

Dad stared up at me for a moment, then turned to his personal *capo*. "Could you please ask Toby to fetch Vincent?"

This guy was the Toby to my dad's Vincent. I'd rarely seen Dad without him in all the years I'd been alive. "Of course." Just like Toby, nothing ruffled him.

"Is this because of the Prestons?" I demanded. "Is this why Vincent's playing monkey in the middle with a bunch of packages? Huh?"

Nobody knew who had killed Dmitri Preston, or caused the disappearance of Alexander Preston. I had a feeling Vincent knew and I'd always thought he'd dealt with the matter quietly to avoid a fuss. But if it was his reason for this warmongering, if he'd gotten my girl kidnapped...

Dad stood up and I could feel the temperature in the room drop by a few degrees.

"Stop throwing a temper tantrum like a child," he hissed.

"Oh, because you would've been calm if Mom had been taken," I snapped.

"Yes, I would have," Dad snapped right back. "Because destructive anger would not help her. Anger should be like a knife—sharp and cold. Not this petty whining."

"I'm not *whining* you crusty son of a bitch," I snarled. I jabbed at the photographs, the photographs showing a disoriented and tied up Kennedy. A Kennedy who, for now—just for now—had all of her limbs. "You put my girlfriend in danger. And I want you to take it, and *me*, seriously!"

"There are other girls," Dad said dismissively. "You of all people should know that."

"She's *mine*. I don't want any other girls, I want *her*. I finally settle down with someone, that thing you're always telling me to do, and you don't care? You don't care that she's innocent?"

"She's not family."

"She could be." The moment I said it, I knew it was true. I wanted Kennedy forever.

Dad scoffed, disbelieving. "She is not that special."

"Mom was that special you fucking hypocrite!"

"Okay," Vincent drawled carefully, inserting himself in between us. I hadn't even heard him come into the room. "How about some deep breaths? From the sound of all the fucking yelling I thought Dante was up here."

Dante and Dad were usually the ones going at it with hammer and tongs, it was true. Until they'd decided to just not really talk at all. The two of them had expertly avoided each other at the wedding, always managing to be on opposite sides of the room.

"Kennedy's been taken by the Petrovs," I snapped at Vincent. "That's what happened. Snatched right out from under us at the goddamn wedding."

"Brazen," Vincent murmured. He picked up the photographs and examined them. "They're sending a message, all right. They can get to us anywhere—and they don't respect us."

"We need to find them," I said. "We're not going to let them hurt her."

Vincent drummed his fingers on the desk and looked at Dad.

Dad shook his head. "I think we should let them kill her."

"They're not going to *kill* her," I growled. "They're going to chop her up into little pieces."

"Then we let them do that," Dad replied, cold as ever. "She is not family and we cannot let the Petrovs, or anyone, lead us around by our balls like this. We can spin this in our favor."

"Undermining the Chinese by freeing their workers… kidnapping a Russo girl and killing her…" Vincent nodded. "Yeah, it'll look like they're unraveling. It would further the idea that they're out of control. I think the families would unite somewhat and go against them."

"This is *insane*," I snapped. "You can't fuckin' destroy the Petrovs."

"No, of course not. But you can cripple them. Weaken them."

"And in turn," my father said with delight,

"you strengthen yourself. The Italians once owned this city. I want to see to it that we own it again."

"Not at the expense of Kennedy," I said. "She's not a pawn to be sacrificed."

"Everyone's a pawn to be sacrificed," Dad countered.

I looked over at Vincent. "Come on, what if it was Marla? You wouldn't let anything happen to her no matter how fucking 'strategically important' it was. You set me up with this package deal and you didn't even tell me everything about it, and now my girl's going to pay the price for it? No fucking way. Stop being the mob *capo* for two seconds and be my damn brother."

"The family business comes before an individual. Marla knows that. She knows that better than anyone."

"Fuck you. Maybe that's why you're in charge and I'm not, but I can't do that. I'd help you get Marla out even if it was stupid. Help me get Kennedy."

Dad spat out something in Italian. Vincent sighed. "Marco, please go take a walk."

"I—"

"Go. Take. A walk."

I glared at Dad, who glared back at me, but I stormed out. Let them discuss pros and cons and crunch numbers like this was a fucking company merger. The temptation to get on my motorcycle and race recklessly through the streets was tempting. Dad had always been worried I'd end up wrapped around a pole just like his brother. What if I got in a bad accident and it was his own behavior that had pushed me into it?

You're better than that. A voice in my head that sounded a lot like Kennedy spoke.

A few months ago, I wouldn't have believed that I could be better. I would've thought that fulfilling all the bad things my father thought about me was all that I could be. I would've pushed myself to annoy him and damn the consequences to myself.

But Kennedy believed in me. She stood up for me. When she looked at me… she didn't see the stupid reckless middle child, the Russo boy that everyone wrote off. She saw someone worth caring about, someone worth respecting.

I wanted to be the person she saw in me.

So I didn't get on my motorcycle. I took a walk.

I could feel someone—probably Toby—following me at a distance, but I didn't acknowledge them. Made sense that Vincent would have someone on me to make sure I wasn't attacked by a Petrov or that I didn't actually go and do anything stupid.

I'd circled the block a couple times when my phone buzzed with a text from Vincent. *Come back up.*

For all my complaining, I was usually a good *soldato*. I followed orders to pick up, deliver, kill, disappear, organize, oversee, or whatever else I was asked. And that instinct was still there. I put my phone back into my pocket and I returned to my father's office.

Dad was no longer there. Vincent stood in front of the desk, photographs of Kennedy in his hand as he examined them.

"Where'd the old man go?" I asked.

Vincent put the photographs down. "I sent him to lunch. It helps improve his mood. So. We have less than twenty-four hours to get this going before they start sending us pieces of her."

I stared at him. "You're... actually helping me?"

"As if you wouldn't go and try to find her on your own and probably get yourself killed." Vincent paused. "I explained to our father that if we just let the Petrovs kill her, we look like we don't care about our own. They snatched her out from right under our noses, so it's only fair that we show our own strength and snatch her right back from under theirs."

My chest felt tight. "Thanks," I said gruffly.

Vincent shrugged. "He just has to be spoken to in a language he understands. And you're my brother. Now." He tapped the desk. "Let's remind these bastards who we are."

A slow, vicious smile spread over my face.

CHAPTER 18

Kennedy

You didn't live and work as a woman in a man's field without learning how to deal with the men.

I'd learned to ignore a lot. To put up with a lot. To work harder and faster and better, to be the top of my class, to prove that I belonged. Even now, in the twenty-first century, law enforcement was not kind to its women.

But on the other side of that, it meant that

I'd learned how to rile men up. How to get their attention in the wrong kind of way. How to make them *angry*.

I wasn't going to let myself be slowly cut to pieces. And I was sure that Marco wouldn't agree to the Petrov demands. Or at the least, his brother and father wouldn't let him, and they were the ones really in charge. That meant that my only option was to goad Misha into killing me quickly.

And boy, had that been easier than I'd expected.

I think it was that Misha really didn't expect a woman to come at him like this. He was used to men and their various possible reactions—the pleading and begging, the stoic silence, the bravado and sass. I chipped away at him using the psychological techniques the bureau had taught me.

I wasn't a profiler, or anything like that. But we all learned a bit about that kind of thing. And we all had to know how to read people on the fly, especially when we were undercover. Misha was a consummate professional. He cared about doing his job well, and he cared about being of value to his bosses. Not his bosses here in America but the ones in Russia who'd sent him over to do the enforcing that others couldn't or wouldn't.

So that's what I attacked.

"Do you know who I am?" I asked him pleasantly as the hours ticked by.

Misha wasn't the type to impatiently pace. He just sat back and played solitaire. "A stripper at Cozy Bunny. But if you think that you'll be able to seduce me into letting you go..." He waggled a finger at me and then turned over another card. "You're mistaken. You wouldn't be the first person to offer me sex, or even to become my permanent bed warmer, if I spared them."

I snorted. "Wow, you really should do your research more. Y'know they said in the file on you that you could stand to be taken down a peg and I guess they were right."

Misha looked up at me slowly. "The file?" he repeated.

I tilted my head at him and smiled, wiggling my fingers. "Hi, dumbass. I'm Special Agent Kennedy Lancaster of the FBI."

Misha exploded, as I'd expected him to.

See, no mafia guy was going to let a cop of any kind leave his care alive. That wasn't how it worked. At first, Misha hoped that he could get information out of me about my Russo operation, but I didn't let anything slip. I was doing this so that I wouldn't betray Marco, and that meant to the Russians as well as to my own people.

Instead, I goaded him. I knew how he'd take it. The idea of this fed, not just any fed but a *woman*, talking back to him like this? Being so high and mighty, talking down to him like he was nothing? Picking at all the ways that he wasn't properly professional, all the ways that he'd fucked up?

Yeah, he couldn't possibly handle that.

I knew more about him than many at the bureau, since the mafia was my division and I needed to be prepped for my undercover work, so I was aware of the sort of jobs he'd done and his position in the family. It was far too easy to needle him about that.

"Word has it, you weren't sent here because you could keep a couple of lazy spoiled brats in line," I spit at him. "Word is that you were sent here because you weren't good enough, weren't *tough* enough, for Russia. Americans are weak, spoiled, you're tough to *them,* but the ones back in Russia know the truth—"

That was when he hit me.

Excellent.

I spat out blood, my ears ringing and my jaw aching. "My boss was right. You're just a thug underneath it all."

The hits kept coming.

I cried, a little. Or rather I should say that some tears fell. I didn't cry. But when you're getting your ass kicked, and you're in pain, tears tend to happen. It's just a biological response. I didn't try to fight it. I just needed to keep him angry enough to kill me *fast.*

Maybe if my parents had still been alive, I wouldn't have done this. Maybe if I'd had any close friends left, if I hadn't lost all of them as taking care of my mom swallowed my whole life, I wouldn't have done this. But I had no one. No one in my life besides Marco. And this—this was all I could do for him. I couldn't be with him. But I could die for him.

I spat out more blood, one of my eyes swollen shut, my head pounding, bruises everywhere. The ropes cut into my wrists and ankles as I jolted around from being hit. My ribs ached.

Misha walked over to the table where he'd been playing solitaire and picked up his gun, cocking it. "I hate to go back on my word," he said, walking back over to me. "But I'm sure Marco will understand when I tell him. A snake like you could not be permitted to live."

"Honor among thieves?" I chuckled, my lips barely able to form the words. They'd split some time ago, and my jaw had been hit, and so forming words was a study in pain.

Misha raised his gun. "More than your kind have."

I closed my eyes, strangely at peace with all of this.

A shot rang out.

There were some who theorized that the moment of death felt like nothing. That one second you were alive and feeling pain, the next—just, all of it gone.

At first, I thought that's what had happened, but then I realized I still felt things. My body still hurt. I just—hadn't been shot?

I opened my good eye.

Misha had a bullet right through the center of his head. He swayed on the spot, like his body was taking a moment to catch up to the idea that he was dead—and then he fell with a sick, heavy thud.

My breathing started to come in fast and shaky. What was this? What was going on?

"Kennedy?" I heard Marco in the distance.

No. No, no, no—no I couldn't go back to him, back to the man I'd be forced to betray, or who'd find out who I was and have to kill me—I couldn't do it.

It was so odd that now was the time I panicked. My breathing turned into hyperventilation and tears leaked out the corners of my eyes. I'd been able to handle Misha no problem, the pain no problem, but the idea that I might have to go back to the terrible choice I thought I'd escaped—that was what got to me.

I couldn't hear any footsteps. If this was a police raid, I'd hear shouts of *clear* and heavy footfalls, but whoever else was with Marco—and I hoped to God he hadn't come alone—made no sound as they investigated the area.

If there were any other goons around, and I was sure there must be, they would never see the Russo team coming.

"Kennedy." Marco hurried around the chair and came into view. His gun was in his hands, and I knew without asking that he'd been the one to fire just now and kill Misha.

I tried to speak, but it just came out as a sob. I hated that I was crying. I had struggled my whole life to be strong—as I lost my father, as I took care of my mother, as I became a federal agent—and now I was falling apart, and for such a stupid reason.

Marco looked around as if to make sure the coast was clear and then tucked his gun away. "Son of a bitch," he snarled under his breath. His eyes blazed. He looked like a wolf on the hunt. "I killed him way too quick."

His fingers hooked gently under my chin and lifted my head, ever so carefully turning it this way and that to examine the damage in the light. Even as his eyes continued to burn with fury, his voice was feather soft. "It's okay now, baby. I've got you. Let's cut you loose and I'll take you home."

He flicked open a wicked sharp knife

and began to expertly cut away at the ropes that held me. Now that I was crying I couldn't seem to stop, and Marco continued to make quiet, soothing noises as he freed me.

I wondered what most people would think to see bad boy Marco Russo being the definition of gentle with me, gently pulling away the ropes that held me and rubbing circulation back into my hands and feet.

"You must've really pissed him off," Marco noted. "Never heard of Misha losing control like that." Pride slid into his eyes. "Atta girl."

In my state of adrenaline, I couldn't hold the truth back. And I didn't want to anymore. I didn't want to hide from him. "It was so he'd kill me quickly."

Marco's gaze went sharp. "Why would you want that?"

"Because I knew Antonio and Vincent wouldn't let you give into the Petrov demands. You can't—be weak." Without the ropes holding me up I realized how dizzy and weak I was, and I slumped forward.

Marco caught me and held me in his arms. "Of course I came for you, baby.

Nobody takes my girl. I'm always going to come for you, keep you safe."

I weakly clutched at his shirt, unable to resist resting my head on his shoulder, breathing in the scent of motor oil and leather that always clung to him. "But you weren't *supposed* to," I whispered. "You were supposed to let me die."

CHAPTER 19

Marco

"*You were supposed to let me die.*"

Kennedy's words were soft, but they echoed in my head, rang in my ears, ricocheted through my chest. What the hell was that supposed to mean? "Like fuck I'd ever let you die."

At that, Kennedy seemed to lose all control and she wept even harder, her breathing hysterical. I'd never seen her like this, never seen her so broken down. I wanted to resurrect Misha and murder him all over again, properly this time, *slowly*, so that he begged for forgiveness for what he'd done to her.

"But you *have* to." Kennedy didn't sound completely… all right.

After a beating like that, yeah, I wasn't surprised. She needed rest, recovery, a doctor's appointment. Maybe some therapy.

"You don't understand—I needed to—to die, it would hurt—hurt you—less."

"Losing you would hurt me less? Hurt me less than what?" I knelt on the floor, Kennedy in my arms. I knew I should get up, carry her out of there, but I somehow couldn't move. She was still in her beautiful yellow dress from the wedding, now stained with her own blood.

"Than my betrayal," Kennedy whispered.

She raised her head slowly to look me in the eye. "I wanted to die loyal to you. Because —because—if I'm alive—I have to betray you."

My body went cold. "Betray me to whom?"

A tear slid out from Kennedy's swollen

eye. "My real last name is Lancaster. Kennedy Lancaster. I'm an FBI agent."

I stared down at her, my mouth hanging open. I was pretty fucking sure I could say I had never been so shocked in my entire life.

As if that had taken the last bit of energy out of her, Kennedy's eyelids fluttered and then slid closed, her body becoming heavy and limp in my arms as she lost consciousness.

Shit. I hauled her up. I was alone, thank fuck. Nobody else had heard what she said. So long as she kept her mouth shut while she got medical attention, maybe we could wait and deal with this privately, just the two of us.

Footsteps sounded—the fact that I could hear them meant that the place was clear. Our guys were good and understood the meaning of stealth, unlike police who just thundered in everywhere declaring themselves.

I stood up, Kennedy still in my arms, her head gently cradled against my shoulder. "She needs medical attention," I told Toby as he came into view.

Vincent was a *capo* which meant he rarely conducted such raids himself, but often sent Toby in his place.

"We'll get her to the doctor," Toby assured me. He eyed her. "That's not Misha's usual method. What happened?"

"I think she pissed him off," I said.

"That was stupid of her."

"Kennedy's not stupid," I replied. "She probably knew our policy would be not to come for her. A quick death's better than a slow one."

Technically, I wasn't lying. I was just conveniently leaving out the part where she'd wanted to die so that she wouldn't have to hurt me by betraying me.

She's not family, Dad had said, multiple times. Vincent had said it too. But what could possibly prove her to be family more than this? She'd wanted to die to keep me safe. To keep my entire *family* safe.

Toby seemed to accept my answer. "Tough cookie."

"You have no idea."

Hell, I barely had an idea, apparently.

We got her to one of our trusted doctors,

who patched her up. Kennedy started to wake up during the process, but he gave her a sedative. I thought it would be better for her to wake up at my place, somewhere she felt safe, rather than at a strange backroom doctor's office.

The doc gave me some ointment and medication for her injuries, and sent us on our way. They're no-nonsense, our doctors. They know that we prefer the school of "shake it off" medicine.

I laid Kennedy carefully down in my bed, got an ice pack for her swollen eye, and rubbed the ointment on her bruises. She'd taken some real hits there. But when I'd been creeping into the building, I hadn't heard a peep from her. No sounds of crying or begging or screaming.

She'd held up. Like a true mafia girl.

The elevator slid open just as I finished up with her bruises. It was Vincent with Toby.

And neither looked happy.

"Finally finished looking into your girl," Vincent said quietly. I stood up. "Jade over at Cozy Bunny had the craziest story to tell me, about a client Kennedy took on before she went steady with you."

I could remember that time. The older man. I'd been seeing red with jealousy.

"The story that Jade told me, is that she had someone check in on your girl, just to make sure everything was okay since they'd never seen the man before. And what does she hear but that this woman isn't giving a lap dance or anything else at all. Instead she'd been giving the guy information. Information about *us*."

Vincent's eyes went dark and I saw our father in him, as our father lives in us all: that dark, swirling, menacing anger that pulses through our blood.

"She's a fed," I said quietly. "I know."

Vincent stared at me. His fingers flexed and I realized his hands were gloved. So. That was why he'd come here. Gloves didn't leave fingerprints.

"How do you know," he said. "When."

"Earlier. She told me before she passed out." I took a subtle step to my right, putting myself directly between Vincent and Kennedy, helpless on the bed. "She wanted to die back there so that she wouldn't be forced to give me, or anyone else in our family, up to her boss. I think we can turn her."

Vincent's tone held no humor. "You think your dick is really that magical."

"What really happened with Marla and her brothers?" I countered. "I know that you've let people believe the Petrovs were responsible so you're justified in your little meddling you've been up to, but if the Petrovs were involved you know I'd know about it. Something happened, and I have a feeling that something led to Marla choosing you."

I stepped forward, just a little bit, just enough. "Kennedy's chosen me. I don't care where she's from."

"And how much might she have already passed along to her boss?" Vincent countered. "We have to punish these things. The feds have to know they can't fuck with us."

"Then keep her on our side," I replied. "If we turn her, that's just as devastating, isn't it?"

Toby was already shaking his head. I wasn't sure why, until Vincent answered for me. After so many years as Vincent's right-hand man, Toby and my brother could practically speak for one another in times like these.

"They'd never let her live," Vincent explained. "They'd consider it a betrayal. Same as if we had a rat in our nest. We'd have to take him out, and they're going to take *her* out."

"So, what, that's it? We have to take her out first, then?"

I didn't realize my voice was rising until I heard Kennedy stir on the bed behind me. She started to sit up, wincing, and I went to sit next to her. "Hey, it's okay baby, take it easy."

Kennedy looked at me, then at Vincent and Toby, through her one good eye. "You know," she said to the other two.

"I didn't tell them," I interrupted her. "They found out—someone looked in on your talk with your boss at the club."

Kennedy sighed and pressed the ice to her eye. "I knew he shouldn't have come. It was reckless and put me in danger. But he's a micromanager."

"You know what we have to do," Vincent said.

Kennedy swallowed hard, then nodded in resignation.

"No," I snapped. "We don't have to do anything. This is my girlfriend we're talking about. I'm not going to let you just, what, fucking kill her?"

"We all know what happens to feds who turn," Kennedy said softly.

"We can protect you," I replied. I looked at Vincent, near desperation. "Can't we? C'mon, who are we if we can't protect the people we love?"

Kennedy made a small, startled noise in the back of her throat, and I cursed myself for not fucking saying anything sooner. I wasn't exactly one for romantic speeches but I should've said something. I didn't want the first time she heard me say that I loved her to be angry and in front of others, not even directed at her.

Vincent's expression didn't change. "Then what the hell do you suggest? This is a no-win scenario, Marco."

I stood up again and loomed as only I

knew how to. "You try to touch one goddamn hair on her head and I'll knock you flat, Vincent. Don't fucking try me."

Vincent could hold his own in a fight. He was a Russo, of course he could. But he wasn't the one who spent every day brawling, hauling in men who didn't want to be hauled anywhere, fighting off rival gangs. He wasn't the one who trained every day in the school of hard knocks down by the docks, getting his knuckles bloody.

Between the two of us, I was pretty sure I could take him.

Vincent stared me down. He knew I might be able to beat him. Vincent wasn't one of those idiots who thought nothing could touch him. He knew the risks, and he knew my skill, at least with my fists.

"I can tell you what I know," Kennedy offered quickly. "The D.A. is planning something. That's why there's a lot of pressure on my case. On me. I don't know what's happened but our plan has changed and now they want me to get information on you guys quickly so they can move."

Vincent looked at Toby, who immediately

pulled out his phone. I knew what he was doing—letting our lawyer brother Dante know that it was finally time to prove his loyalty. That had been the condition of allowing him to become a lawyer.

You never escaped family.

"I think that there's more they aren't telling me," Kennedy added. "To be fair, I haven't told them a lot. I didn't tell them anything about the package plan or how you're turning two families against each other, Vincent. But they're keeping me in the dark about something. I don't know what."

"You think that's enough information to be useful?" Vincent asked. "You think that I can trust you when you say you haven't told them anything?"

I glared at my brother. I never thought that it would come to this. I'd never thought that anyone or anything could make me truly go up against Vincent. But turned out, love was a bitch that way. I'd do anything to protect Kennedy. And I knew she hadn't given me up. I could feel it in my bones.

"Let me call my boss," Kennedy said

quickly. “Tell him that you suspect me, that Marco beat me up.”

A low growl sounded in my throat. I’d never beat my girlfriend, ever. Even if it was true and she had betrayed me, even if she’d been playing me this whole time. I just couldn’t allow that.

“You can listen in,” Kennedy said. “And based on what my boss says, we can move from there. He might ask me to pressure you for more information before I go, or he might ask me to do something to prove my loyalty to you. But whatever he says, I might be able to get him to let something slip about their bigger plans, about their partnership with the D.A.”

Vincent looked at Kennedy for a long moment. Then he looked at me.

I glared back at him. I didn’t want to fight my brother. Annoyed with one another we might get, but actually fighting? On opposite sides? I never would’ve thought it would happen, and I didn’t want it to.

For Kennedy, though, I’d do it.

Vincent sighed. “Let’s see what I can dig up, and how this conversation will go.” He wasn't speaking to Kennedy, but to me, and I knew it. "This isn't a pardon. Not yet. It's a delay in execution."

Kennedy winced, then nodded in understanding.

I swallowed hard. Vincent wasn't doing this to spare someone's life or because he had any faith in Kennedy. He was doing this for me. "Thank you."

"Don't make me regret it," Vincent replied.

He turned and Toby followed him back to the elevator.

CHAPTER 20

Kennedy

The moment that his brother left, Marco relaxed. He sat down on the edge of the bed again and took my hand. "How are you feeling?"

"I ache all over," I admitted. There was no point in being brave now. I was sure my face looked a mess. "But I'm not dead."

"No, you're not." A shadow passed over Marco's features.

"Why didn't you let him kill me?" I asked

softly. I didn't understand. Marco said he loved me. That he'd protect me from his own brother. But I had lied to him this entire time.

"You tried to get yourself killed so that I wouldn't ever know the truth," Marco replied. "Not out of selfish reasons. Because you didn't want me to feel betrayed by you. You didn't want to hurt me like that. That kind of love and loyalty can't... it can't be bought or found easily and I don't..."

He cleared his throat. "I've never felt like this about anyone and I don't know if I ever will again. And I don't think that... the kind of loyalty you've shown is something I should give up. I don't think a woman like you should be given up if you're the guy lucky enough to have her."

I swallowed. "You're nothing like what I was told to expect in my briefing. I thought you'd be... so much less of a man. I thought you'd be stupid and violent and untrustworthy. But you were... you *are* everything."

Marco didn't look at me, instead looking down at our joined hands. Like he wasn't quite sure if he'd be able to handle looking at me dead-on, like I was the sun and I'd blind him.

"I really didn't want to hurt you," I whispered. "I wanted you to never know. Because I… I've never felt like this, either and it terrifies me, but all I know is that I want to be loyal to you. Always."

"Don't know if you noticed this, sweetheart, but you're a fed." Marco's voice was tired. His thumb traced circles along the back of my hand. "Aren't I the enemy?"

"I don't think that you're any better or worse than cops," I admitted. "I've seen how you take care of me, and take care of your own. I respect your brother, and I like your sister-in-law. And I…" I took a deep breath. "I've been alone, ever since my mother died. She was sick for so long, I lost touch with everyone I'd ever called a friend, taking care of her. And then in the academy, you don't make friends. Especially if you're a woman. You're too busy trying to be the best and prove yourself. There's nobody in my life."

I leaned forward, wincing a little as the action pulled on my various bruises and cuts, and took Marco's chin in my hand. I tilted his face up so that his dark eyes met mine. "There's only you. And if it's choosing between two groups, and one of them has the man I love in it… then it's not really a choice. Not to me. It's you, every time."

Marco cleared his throat, then took my hand in his and pressed his mouth to my knuckles. A thrill ran up my arm. There was more passion in that touch just then than I'd gotten in actual sex from previous boyfriends. He kissed my hand like he was asking for benediction.

"Nobody's ever chosen me before," he admitted at last, his voice so low I could barely hear it. "I've always been… a disappointment."

"Not to me," I promised.

Marco turned my hand over and kissed the inside of my wrist, his lips against my thudding pulse. "I'll tear them all apart," he growled.

His eyes flashed like a wolf's. I felt like if I could see all of his teeth in that moment, they would be sharp, every last one of them. "None of them will hurt you. Not the feds and not my family."

"It won't come to that." Or at least I hoped it wouldn't. "We'll do reconnaissance, and we'll figure out how to handle Johnson and the others."

Marco pushed himself up and wrapped a supportive arm around my waist. His lips ghosted over the corner of my mouth, like he knew he had to be gentle with me but he also couldn't resist touching me like this.

I gripped his shoulders, hanging onto him like a buoy in a raging sea.

"We'll get through this," Marco promised me. "You and me, we'll get through this."

"I've never trusted anyone like I've trusted you," I admitted.

So I trusted him when he told me we'd find a way.

The next few days, I spent recovering. Vincent and I both argued that it would be best if we acted now while my bruises were still fresh, but Marco argued that he wasn't going to send me into another dangerous situation when I was still on bed rest. Eventually I was convinced to see things Marco's way when the ever-helpful Toby pointed out that the extent of my beating was too severe for the story I was telling my supervisor. Misha had been beating me in order to kill me. Marco was supposed to have just knocked me around a little to test me. Johnson, or really anyone with any common sense, would be able to tell the difference and would wonder how the hell I got out of that situation alive.

So we waited, while I stopped looking less like a murder victim and more like a woman who'd just taken a couple punches.

I kept waiting for Marco's behavior to change. For him to show some kind of sign that he was wary or angry around me now. But it never came. He looked at me the way he always had.

There was only so long I could handle that before I was ready to burst.

One thing that helped with my recovery was nice hot soaks in the balcony jacuzzi. One evening Marco joined me, and I took advantage of the opportunity.

"Why don't you hate me?" I asked.

Marco stared at me as he got into the jacuzzi. He was powerful, thick muscle from head to toe, his colorful tattoos standing out from his tanned Italian skin. He still made my mouth water every time and I was annoyed that I wasn't quite fit enough to be up for our usual athletic sex.

"Why would I?" he asked.

He walked through the water towards me, drops sliding down his skin. He was power personified and I couldn't resist sliding my hands up his chest, pressing down, feeling the muscles.

"Because I lied to you that whole time. I was a fed and I was planning to help take your whole family down. There's got to be some anger about that, right?"

Marco snorted. "Did you actually give them anything to take us down?"

"…no?"

His hands slid under my thighs and he gently lifted me up, turning us around so that as he settled down on the step, I was on his lap. His hands moved up and down my back, soothing, almost but not quite massaging.

"You were willing to die for me, Kennedy. That's not something I take lightly. If you'd told me before… I would've been angry. But what the fuck were you supposed to do, huh? Tell me right away and I would've killed you. Wait too long and I'd kill you for betraying me. You were stuck between a rock and a hard place. And now..." Marco kissed my mostly healed jaw. "You couldn't have done more to prove your allegiance. Not in my eyes."

"Your brother needs more convincing."

"My brother did something for his wife. Or she did something for him. I don't know, but it was big. He might not trust you but he understands how I feel. I know that much. And I know you'll prove yourself to him once we take care of your boss."

A dark look passed over Marco's face. "Your boss is the one who needs to pay. He met you in the damn club. Like he didn't trust you. That's how you were found out."

I swallowed. "I wondered—but I figured Jade wouldn't have anyone watching if I didn't request anyone to watch. It was a calculated risk."

"Too big of a risk. If he really cared about you, he would've waited for you to be at your apartment or something."

An odd look passed over Marco's face, and he muttered again, "If he really cared…"

"What is it?" I asked.

Marco had that hunting wolf look, the kind he got when he was thinking. Like he'd just caught the scent of a potential deer. "Nothing. We'll see, when you call."

He kissed my neck, not like a prelude to something, more like a little reminder. Like he couldn't help himself.

"Are you sure?" I asked.

"I'm sure. We'll see later."

I nodded. I trusted him this far, I could trust him with whatever little idea he had brewing in the back of his head. Especially after how I'd been working against him this whole time. I traced his tattoos with my fingers. "You know… I am feeling better."

Marco gave me a firm look. "You've still got bruises."

"But they don't stop me from moving." It was true. I didn't really ache anymore. I still looked fairly bad when I looked into the mirror but it had all healed enough that I could move around without wincing.

I lightly drew my nails down his chest. I'd

missed having sex with him. Going to sleep curled around him every night was delightful, his strong arms making me feel safe and secure. But I missed having him inside of me. I missed his hot, hard kisses, his tongue on my body. And even when he said he trusted me, I had a way to show him that I trusted him. A way to show him that I was his, completely.

"Kennedy." Marco lightly wrapped his hands around my wrists. "I don't want to aggravate your damn injuries."

"You won't." I squirmed in his lap, and Marco's face flushed. I could feel him getting hard against me, swelling in the tight black underwear he'd worn into the hot tub. Marco rarely bothered with wearing anything at all in his own private jacuzzi. "There's… there's something I've always wanted to do, with a partner, something I've never done before. Because I never trusted my partners enough."

Marco arched an eyebrow at me. "I'll probably still say no. Until you're healed."

I had a feeling he'd change his mind. "I have a little thing for bad boys."

Marco smirked. "Really? I never noticed."

I lightly slapped his shoulder. "But they were also… untrustworthy. I never knew if I'd be able to give them control over me like this."

"Like what?"

I took a deep breath. "I want you to tie me to your bed. And I want you to… to play with me. Make me beg for you. And then I want you to fuck me, just like that."

Marco's eyes went dark and hungry, his jaw clenching. I could feel his cock rubbing against me now, through the fabric of my bathing suit and his briefs.

I could see the thoughts swirling behind his eyes as he calculated. Marco wasn't just an idiot who thought with his dick. I knew that. But he *did* know sex. He'd kept me balanced on a motorcycle, for crying out loud. And I knew he was running over the logistics in his head right that second and realizing that if he tied me up comfortably and properly, my remaining injuries wouldn't be exacerbated. In fact, he'd be able to secure me so I wouldn't really be able to move. I'd be perfectly safe.

A smirk that I wouldn't, a few months

ago, have ever let myself give to Marco Russo flitted across my face. He was hooked, and I knew it.

"Well..." Marco dragged his gaze over my form, cataloguing all of the bruises that still remained on my body. "I suppose I could work with that." He tilted his head and looked at me. "You've never let anyone else do this to you?"

I shook my head. "I've wanted it for... years. But I never trusted my partner. Or I knew he wouldn't want to do it so I never even bothered asking."

The girl who had dated a fellow FBI agent, the most strait-laced one I could find, felt like another person. I never would settle for that kind of man now. Not with Marco in front of me, ready to take me.

Marco considered me for another moment. I could practically feel the hunger inside of him, barely held back by ropes and chains of common sense, inches away from breaking free.

Finally, he cursed under his breath. I grinned in triumph, not even bothering to hide my glee at my success.

"If we're about to go up against the feds," he said, "then I want to take advantage of being with you before the shit hits the fan."

With that, his hands slid under my thighs and he hoisted me up, guiding me to wrap my legs around him as he stood and exited the hot tub.

Warm water cascaded down from our bodies, dripping onto the floor as he carried me inside, first to the bathroom to dry me off and strip away my swim suit and his briefs, then across the penthouse to his massive bed. It was a good thing I was tall, and a good thing that he probably had something nice and long to tie me up with, or I would've been too small to be stretched the expanse of the California king.

Marco gently laid me down on the mattress, more gently than he would have normally I was sure, as ever careful of my injuries. "Scoot up onto the pillows," he ordered.

His voice was dipping down into that darker, dripping-dark-chocolate register that had electricity shooting up and down my spine every time. I shivered and did as I was told.

Marco knelt down and pulled out one of the drawers that made up the base of the bed. I heard him rummaging around in it, and a moment later he stood back up.

In his hands were now some bright red silk ties, and a pair of fuzzy handcuffs.

I swallowed, my mouth dry. It was finally happening. My body was already beginning to shake in anticipation. All of my years of fantasizing alone as I touched myself, and it was all coming to this.

"Hands above your head," Marco instructed softly.

I did as I was told, and Marco walked around to the head of the bed. He carefully wrapped the handcuffs around my wrists, the soft black fur gentle against my skin. He hooked the handcuffs around the slats of the headboard, then cuffed my other hand.

"How's it feel?" he stared at me with fire in his eyes, like he couldn't wait to devour me and was forcing himself to hold back.

I tested the hold, then rotated my wrists. "It feels secure."

The cuffs weren't too tight. They weren't so loose I'd hurt myself by accidentally yanking out of them, either. I felt… something inside of me settle as I realized that I was well and truly caught up in these cuffs. My heart raced with excitement and my pussy practically pulsed with desire and anticipation, but I also felt this odd sense of serenity wash over me. Like finally something was clicking into place, the empty, craving space filled.

"Good," Marco whispered. He ran the backs of his knuckles along the curve of my cheek, then moved down to the foot of the bed. "Spread your legs."

I did as I was told and immediately, Marco's expert hands began to wind the red silk ties around my ankles. He'd done this before, as I'd suspected he had. Marco was never one to skimp out on a possible sex toy, never one to leave an option unexplored.

After a moment, I realized that he was binding my ankles the way that you would bind up a wrap for a sprain. He was tying me up as I'd requested but he was doing it in a way that would support my ankles and keep them from getting hurt. Part of me was fascinated by the skill used—and part of me melted, knowing that he was looking out for me like this. Still determined to make sure I was taken care of.

Once my ankles were secure, Marco wrapped the other end of the silk ties around something underneath the bed. Possibly one of the drawers? Or was there some kind of hook or knob specifically for this purpose? I wouldn't have put it past him.

Marco inspected his work. "Test them for me," he ordered.

His voice was both soft and sharp, orders that I knew I would obey, but orders I also knew I would trust.

I tested them as he requested and nodded my approval. The ties held me tightly without tugging harshly at my ankles the way the ties that Misha used had done. A rush of gratitude swept through me for the care Marco was taking. These weren't ties meant to subdue me harshly or hold me in place like a prisoner. They were meant to hold me steady and secure, to keep me from hurting myself—to hold me in place for pleasure.

I knew that I had been right in thinking I could trust Marco with this. That finally that itch deep inside of me would be scratched.

Marco's gaze swept over me, checking in on his handiwork, and then he nodded. "You've been really pent up these last few days."

"So have you," I pointed out, eyeing his already hard cock.

Marco smirked at me, and I saw him settle into that predatory, hunting look he got when we were in bed together. The wolf was out to play.

He moved up my body, and even though he was technically crawling, it didn't feel like it. It felt like on all fours was how he was meant to move, his natural element, not crawling but *stalking*.

My breath hitched. My skin felt alive, sparking, every inch of me ten times more sensitive just from the amount of anticipation I felt.

Marco lowered himself down and I thought he was going to kiss me—but then he ducked his head at the last moment and kissed me softly, slowly, on the neck.

"Y'know, a less generous man would take advantage of this situation," he pointed out. "After you lied to me all this time... pretended to be someone you're not..."

"Oh?" My voice came out soft and breathy.

"Maybe I should really take my time with you." I could hear the tease in Marco's voice as he slowly kissed his way across my shoulder. "Make you *earn* your orgasm."

I shivered. That was what I wanted, desperately. I wanted to be strung out and begging, my mind completely blissed out. But I'd never before trusted whoever was in charge to do it right. How could I know, once I was tied up, that my partner would stop if I asked them to? How could I know they wouldn't do something I didn't like, or would hurt me, or refuse to untie me?

Sure, I was trained somewhat in how to escape from these kinds of things but depending on the type of restraint used or what knots they employed... it was really just something I hadn't wanted to risk.

But I knew instinctively that Marco would never do any of that to me. I knew I could trust him—that if I said stop or no, he would immediately end things. That if there was something I didn't like, he wouldn't do it. And that if I asked him sincerely to untie me, he would.

Marco slowly, inexorably kissed his way down my body and I sighed into it, my muscles relaxing. He hadn't stretched my limbs so far that I felt like I was doing any kind of workout. I just sank down into the mattress and pillows, and let myself focus on nothing but the touch of his mouth.

It was glorious.

I had no idea where he would go next, his movements over my skin apparently random. Sometimes he gave me the softest brush of lips, more the promise of a kiss than anything else. Other times he bit into my skin and sucked, making me cry out—like he was trying to give me new, good bruises to help me forget the old, bad ones. Sometimes it was a soft, fond press, other times it was slow and sucking.

I reveled in the attention. I'd never felt like this before—worshipped and devoured at the same time.

Marco moved all the way down to between my thighs, right where I was wet and aching for him. He took his time on my legs, and I hadn't even realized just how goddamn wet I was until I could feel him only inches away. I trembled, wishing I could slide my fingers into his hair and buck my hips to encourage him closer—but I was tied up. Held fast. I couldn't move at all.

The feeling of being restrained, truly held back, hit me like a freight train and I let out a small whimper from the back of my throat. It was a dizzying combination of trust, loss of control, and being at someone else's mercy, at *Marco's* mercy, that had my head spinning like I stood at the edge of the balcony, hundreds of feet above the ground.

Marco avoided my aching pussy and moved up to my stomach. I huffed at him but didn't complain. It was my instinct to be quiet during sex, and I wasn't going to change that unless he really earned it.

I had a feeling he was going to really earn it.

Marco moved up with purpose this time, no feeling around or detours. When his mouth latched around my nipple I bit my lip hard. God, yes, that felt amazing. I struggled to breathe and to keep from yanking too hard on the handcuffs as I instinctively tried to squirm against the touch, to arch up into his mouth.

Marco growled in satisfaction, licking and sucking, nipping occasionally, not content until I was shaking and my breast and nipples swollen from his attention.

Then he switched to the next one.

I panted, my gaze blurring as I writhed under his mouth. I could feel something building at the back of my throat, although what it was, I wasn't sure.

"Goddamn," Marco growled. His voice and gaze were feral. "You're so fucking needy, baby. Look at you."

His finger skimmed slowly up my body to my throat, my chin, hooking underneath and guiding me to look him in the eye. "You're fucking gorgeous like this. The red goes so well with your skin. And in those cuffs…"

He scraped his teeth against my jaw, then nibbled on my ear. "You're fucking *delicious*."

Then, before I could even realize what he

was doing, he was moving down and putting his tongue between my legs.

My body tugged instinctively on the restraints, but of course I couldn't move, and it sent such a thrill through me, the knowledge that I was so helpless as he licked into me—that the thing building at the back of my throat finally released and I moaned his name.

Marco looked up at me, his mouth slick with my arousal, a wicked grin on his lips. "You haven't even *started* begging yet," he promised me, and the shiver that shot through me, full of heat and need, felt unreal.

I was in for the ride of my life, and I was in love with every step of it.

CHAPTER 21

Marco

I grinned as I watched Kennedy shake and tremble underneath my touch. She was so fucking gorgeous spread out like this I could hardly stand it.

I'd never pictured her like this before—I'd never dared. Of course I'd had fun like this with some former flings of mine, but Kennedy was so much her own woman, so in command of herself, that I'd thought even with her kinky streak she wouldn't possibly want to give into me *this* much.

Looked like I'd been wrong. And I'd never been so goddamn glad to be proven wrong about something.

Every inch of Kennedy's skin, those miles of legs, her tight hot curves, were on display for me. They were bare to my mercy. And I had every intention of taking my time.

I moved back between her legs and licked at her, tasting the slick sensation of her arousal on my tongue, heavy with promise. Kennedy's body strained to touch me in return, and her breathing grew harsher as she was held back.

God, it was unbelievably sexy to have this power over her, to be able to tease and touch her like this. I could hardly stand it. My cock was so goddamn hard, I wanted to fuck her right now, just like this, but I held back. I wanted her to completely surrender to me and fall apart and that wouldn't happen if I rushed this.

Perhaps there was a part of me that wanted to drag this out a bit because she had lied to me, hidden the truth of her identity from me. But this wasn't punishment. I could tell that this was something she wanted, that this was something she'd been craving, yearning to have, an itch that had never been scratched. And I wanted, more than anything in that moment, to give that to her.

I licked at her folds and twisted my tongue inside of her, avoiding her clit until I could feel her entire body straining with desire—and then pulling away.

The look of fire in Kennedy's eyes was intoxicating. She was quiet in bed, which normally I didn't mind. But I was sure I could get her to beg for me. I just had to be patient.

Me, patient? Vincent would've laughed. But Kennedy was teaching me to be a better guy. Even if that patience was now showing up most predominantly in the bedroom.

I winked at her in response and moved down to her ankles, slowly kissing my way back up her legs.

"Marco..." Kennedy whispered, tugging fruitlessly at her bonds. "Marco, *please*..."

"I'm not sure you're really desperate enough." I wanted her practically incoherent by the time I let her come.

I worked my way back up to her dripping pussy and set my mouth on it again. This time, after teasing her for a bit, I sucked on her clit, flicked my tongue against it. I could feel her clenching down, her hips trying to buck up, drawing her so close to climax—

And then I pulled away again.

Kennedy whined, actually whined, this time. I grinned in victory. But I wasn't done yet.

I moved away, back up her body, kissing slowly until I finally got to that beautiful mouth of hers, and kissed her properly, deeply.

Kennedy whimpered up into my mouth and kissed me back. I could feel her putting all of her energy into it, like since the rest of her body was tied down she could only channel everything into this one touch.

I sucked on her tongue, then slid mine into her mouth, gave her the deep kiss she was craving and then pulled back before she could get too comfortable with it. Kennedy gasped in frustration as I pulled away—and then arched as I slid my fingers into her pussy.

"Fuck, yeah, look at you," I murmured as I pumped my fingers deep. "So fucking beautiful… that's it, that's perfect, take it, take what I'm giving you."

Kennedy shuddered. I could tell she wanted to fuck herself on my fingers—but she couldn't. All she could do was lie there and take what I gave her, what I chose to do to her, and it seemed to be driving her fucking wild.

Hell, it was driving me wild, watching her.

I definitely wanted to fuck her, but I was still mindful of her injuries. Kennedy kept insisting she was fine, but I wasn't going to take a chance and hurt her. I knew if our positions were swapped I'd be saying I was fine a hell of a lot sooner than I actually should. I was going to be careful, and I was going to really push her to the edge so that by the time I did fuck her, it wouldn't take long for either of us to come.

I curled my fingers inside of her, fucking her harder with them, and Kennedy began to pant, her body heaving, and just when I thought I could detect a whine beginning to emerge, when I could feel her hot, tight pussy clenching around me—I pulled my fingers out.

Kennedy let out a desperate moan. "*Marco.*"

"What?" I teased, running my wet fingertips lightly up and down her thighs, and along her stomach. "What do you want, baby?"

"I want you to fuck me," she moaned.

"Hmm." I kissed where my fingers had just been—the soft skin of her inner thighs and the barely-there roundness of her stomach. "I'm not sure you want it enough..."

"God, I do, please, please..."

I slid my fingers back into her, accompanying them with my tongue this time, and Kennedy strained, her body wanting to writhe and thrash with sensation but trapped, unable to. It was so fucking delicious to hear her, to see her, completely under my control. It was the hottest goddamn thing I'd ever seen. I had no words for the sensation that thrummed through me as I stared at her.

God, I wanted her more than I'd ever wanted anyone else. I knew in that moment that I was never going to want anyone else ever again.

It was one thing to think, *I'm in love with her.* It was another to realize that this was not just an emotion for the present, but an emotion for always. I was always going to love her. I never wanted to fuck anyone else, to date anyone else, to be with anyone except for Kennedy.

I drove her right up to the edge once again and brought her down, and Kennedy sobbed at the loss. Fuck, she was seriously losing control and it was insanely hot.

I slid back up her body, cupping her face in my hands and kissing her. "I love you," I murmured. I hated that I'd said it for the first time, or at the very least insinuated it, in front of others. That I hadn't said it first to her.

Kennedy sighed into my mouth, a happy, contented little noise. "I love you, too," she replied. As if she needed to say it. As if I didn't already know from the sacrifices she had made for me.

"You know what you want," I whispered

to her. As if there was any doubt that I'd give her what she asked for.

Kennedy nodded.

"Then *beg* me for it," I growled.

The rush that I got when she instantly obeyed was unholy. The dark wolf that lived inside of me triumphed as Kennedy squirmed as much as she could on the bed and moaned, "Please, fuck me, Marco please, *please,* I'm begging you to fuck me, *please* let me come, I need it so badly, please, please, *please—*"

Nobody else had ever gotten her to beg like this. Nobody else had ever had her trust like this. Well, nobody else would earn that chance, now, because I'd done it. I would take care of her, make her into a sobbing wreck and bring her to the biggest goddamn high she'd ever had, the best orgasm she'd ever had, for as long as she'd have me.

I kissed her. "Good girl, I think that was some proper begging. Maybe next time I'll make you go even longer."

Kennedy moaned and when I slid my fingers between her legs, I found she was even wetter than before. Goddamn, this really turned her on—and that turned me on. *Fuck.*

I grabbed a condom from the nightstand and rolled the latex down my aching shaft. I had to squeeze the base of my cock to keep myself from losing it too soon. She was gorgeous, covered in sweat and the marks of my mouth, her long-limbed body stretched out for the taking.

And she was *begging* me to take her.

"Relax for me, baby," I reminded her as I began to slide my cock into her.

Kennedy let out a low moan as I pushed my cock all the way inside. She was so hot and tight, I felt like I was about to go cross-eyed. I speared my fingers through her hair and kissed her again, drinking in the sexy little noises she made. They still weren't that loud, but I reveled in them. It didn't matter that she wasn't a screamer. What mattered was that each whimper and moan was a sign that I'd driven her to the point of desperation. I'd earned each one of her quiet noises, damn it.

For a moment I just stayed inside her, unmoving, getting myself used to it again.

Between her kidnapping and then trying to avoid aggravating her injuries, we hadn't had proper sex in what felt like goddamn ages. It was overwhelming to be inside of her again.

Kennedy clenched around me, whimpering. "Marco, Marco *please.* Please come on, *move, dammit—*"

How was I supposed to resist a plea like that?

I pulled out and thrust back in, going for slow and deep rather than hard and fast. I didn't want to hurt her. The noise that was punched out of Kennedy as I slid all the way back inside her told me I'd made the right choice. Every inch of me sank into her and I groaned, vibrating with pleasure.

"Yes," Kennedy whispered, her eyes nearly dilated with lust. "*Yes,* Marco, yes..."

I slid into her again and again, my hands now braced on either side of her head. I could hardly breathe with the fire roaring inside of me, the triumphant feeling of *mine, mine, mine.* She was letting *me* tie her up and *take* her.

Kennedy continued to beg me under her breath, so desperate to come, on the edge, and I snarled in pleasure. Yes, she was right there, it wasn't going to take much to push her over the cliff…

I shifted my weight and brought my other hand down to rub at her clit and she melted, her body shaking, eyes fluttering as she came around me. It was so fucking hot, she was so tight, I couldn't possibly hold myself back. I felt like I was hit with a goddamn freight train as I came, growling deep in my throat like an animal.

Kennedy and I panted together, our bodies slick with sweat. I felt like my entire body was filled with liquid fire, each breath too sharp, everything a haze. It looked like Kennedy's orgasm went on and on, small noises falling from her lips as she shivered and clenched around me, so tight I felt like I couldn't pull out.

We were definitely going to do this again, if this was the kind of reaction I got from her, the kind of climax she had while being restrained.

Finally, though, I was able to pull out and untie her. It looked like between the type of wrap I'd used for her ankles and the fuzzy handcuffs, she hadn't suffered any bruising. I massaged her arms and legs just to be sure, though. Didn't want her to be full of pins and needles.

Kennedy was practically boneless, staring up at me with pleasure-hazy eyes. "That… was… amazing," she whispered, her words fuzzy around the edges.

"Good." I kissed her. "You were fucking fantastic. Gorgeous."

Tomorrow we had to move forward on this… semi-plan. We had to put Kennedy in danger by contacting her handler. But for now, tonight, there was just the pleasure, and the knowledge that my girl trusted me.

I was going to cling to that for all it was worth.

CHAPTER 22

Kennedy

Toby set up a series of contraptions that would allow everyone to hear what was said on the phone call. I felt like we were on an episode of some crime procedural. I'd worked in the FBI and had done training with this kind of thing, briefly, but I'd never actually been a part of something like this in real life.

I mentioned as much to Marco, who nodded in an oddly quiet fashion, as if he already knew that I would say something like that.

I knew the gears were turning in his head. But I wasn't sure what they were turning *about*.

"We're all set," Toby said, and I picked up my burner phone to give Johnson a call.

I took a deep breath as the phone rang. It answered after four of them. "Hello?"

"Johnson, it's me."

"I figured. Why are you calling? Any big developments?"

I took another deep breath. "Marco suspects something. He... roughed me up a bit. I can send you some pictures, if you'd like. I think I was asking too many questions. It was going really well—I got invited to the wedding and everything but—I think I let my guard down a bit too much."

There was a long pause at the other end of the line, and then Johnson said, "All right. Keep doing what you're doing."

My heart skipped a little in my chest. "... sir? You don't want to pull me out?"

I looked over at Marco. His arms were

folded and his expression was thunderous, but he didn't look at all surprised.

"No," Johnson replied. "You're the only one we've gotten in this far. If we pull you out... Marco's not going to fall for the same trick again and we'll have to start from scratch with a new idea. The D.A.'s certain they've got a case, all you have to do is keep up your work."

"What is my work, exactly?" I asked, impatient. "Because right now it feels like you're setting me up to get caught."

"You'll find a way to allay his suspicions. You're a clever girl."

"And how will my staying with Marco help the D.A.'s case, sir? It sounds like they've got all the information they want without needing any more intel from me. I feel like I'm kind of a moot point, sir." I paused, then added, "With all due respect."

Which was none.

"You're not a moot point, Lancaster, trust me," Johnson replied. "You're the linchpin. Stay on the case and keep trying to get info out of Marco. I'll check in with you in a few days."

He hung up.

I looked over at Marco. So, I noticed, did Toby. He must've sensed it too—that Marco knew something we didn't. That he'd put a piece of the puzzle together.

Marco placed his hand on my shoulder, his thumb stroking back and forth. "Bastard," he said quietly.

"Marco?" Toby asked.

Marco sighed and squeezed my shoulder. "You and I both know, Toby, that my father isn't exactly the cuddliest of men. But have you ever known him to keep someone in a hostile situation like this?"

"No," Toby replied. "Not unless the men knew they were..." He paused, and I saw understanding light up in his eyes.

My stomach sank, even though I couldn't quite say why. "What is it?"

Toby just stared at Marco, obviously letting him take the lead on this one.

"We would pull our men out," Marco said, "Unless they understood that it was a suicide mission."

Instinctively, I shook my head. "No. The

bureau wouldn't do it like that. They'd pull me out if they felt that I was in real danger."

"Send photos of yourself, then," Marco challenged me. "See how seriously he takes your safety."

My fingers shaking a little, I took some selfies of my bruised face and sent them to Johnson. A few minutes later I got a response:

Thank you for the info. Keep at it.

I swallowed hard.

"What's the big thing the DA thinks they have on us?" Marco asked. "Because unless there's something up their sleeve that they're being mighty quiet about, they don't have anything new."

"Mr. Russo's plan to upset the Petrovs and the Chinese dynamics is working," Toby said, "But only he, myself, and Marco here know about it. And none of us squealed."

"And I know that I wasn't tailed by anyone on my package runs," Marco added.

I could certainly believe that. Marco was the best *soldato* the Russo family had, trained by his father and with the Russo ruthlessness running in his veins.

"That means," Marco went on, "that they don't know about our little destabilization efforts. The Petrovs might suspect, which is why they kidnapped you, but we took out Misha and his team, so only the higher-ups know anything and they wouldn't be talking to the DA. So what is this big thing the DA would have planned to take us down?"

The understanding was right there, right at the edge of my brain, but I didn't want to look at it. I didn't want to see the truth.

"Baby." Marco's voice was soft as he sat down and took my hand. "Haven't you wondered why a rookie like yourself with no undercover experience was put on this job?"

My throat was bone dry. I swallowed a few times, my gaze unable to leave Marco's. "They *want* you to find me out," I whispered. "That's why Johnson came to the club. He knew it was sloppy but he was hoping that it would help you to find me out. He wants you to kill me."

"Nothing the public or the law hates more than when the mafia kills an upstanding cop," Toby murmured.

"You'd be a martyr." Marco's fingers

traced over the curve of my cheek, my neck, my shoulder. "Beautiful, young, parents died young, top marks at the academy… the sort of woman that people cry over when she dies. You're perfect for them. They'd use you to get me, and my brother, up on murder charges."

I exhaled shakily and grabbed his hand. "I didn't know. I'd never…"

"Of course you didn't." Toby's voice was bitter. "At least we're honest about the fuckin' blood we spill. You were supposed to be kept in the dark."

He stood up and gathered his equipment. "I'll tell the boss about this."

"Sure thing, Toby." Marco's eyes were black. "And tell him I've already got an idea of how to take care of this business."

Toby paused. "You sure about that? You've never run an operation before."

"This'll be a very simple one," Marco said. "Vincent and dear old Dad want to know they can trust me to be responsible? Well this is me showing them." He looked at me. "I'm responsible for Kennedy. And I'm going to take care of her, and this situation."

Toby nodded. "All right. I'll let him know."

I looked up at Marco as Toby left. "What are you going to do?"

"We're going to do what your handler wants," Marco replied. "We're going to kill you."

CHAPTER 23

Marco

Jade took some persuading. "I don't want my club to be known as a dangerous place for its dancers."

I assured her that this was all staged, and that she was welcome to let everyone know it was staged as long as she ensured they stayed quiet about it to any cops. I didn't care if the rest of our world knew that Kennedy had made it out—I cared that the cops declared her legally dead so that they couldn't do anything about it when she showed up on my arm a few months later.

Kennedy texted her handler again a few days after their phone conversation, telling him that she really didn't feel safe, that I was growing moody and dangerous, and that all of her questions were being shut down. *He has to know who I really am,* she told Johnson. *I'm scared for my life. Marco's violent and unstable.*

She sent this text while lying in my arms in bed, so I snorted at the message contents. Violent? Only to my enemies. Unstable? Definitely not.

The response she received back? *You're so close. We can't pull you out now.*

Fucking prick.

Now it was time. Kennedy was supposed to meet the scumbag at work again, this time through the back alley—the fact that he agreed so readily only confirmed what we already knew. If he'd been a decent handler he would've gotten her from her apartment and bundled her away to safety, say in D.C. but instead, he had her meet him at her place of work. He was hoping she would die there.

Thanks to all of my previous encounters with women of the night, I knew someone who was a wizard with outfits, and we got Kennedy a bullet-proof corset to wear with a pair of cute panties. I wouldn't have trusted some random guy not to go for a headshot, but since this would be me doing the shooting, I knew I'd hit the corset.

Vincent had tried to convince me to give the job to one of our sharpshooters, but I wasn't going to put Kennedy's life in anybody's hands but mine. I loved her. I trusted myself to keep her safe, not some guy just doing it for the money—no matter how loyal to the Russo name he was.

The old guy arrived on time, just like a fuckin' cop, and walked down the alley. From my perch up on the roof I could see him take out his phone. A moment later, Kennedy exited the back door, obviously in receipt of whatever text the guy sent.

"You're not leaving much to the imagination," Johnson said.

We'd put her in that outfit, specifically so that he would know she wasn't wearing a wire. Didn't need to, when we'd put a bug underneath the dumpster right next to them.

"It's my job," Kennedy replied. She did a good job of sounding scared but trying to hide it, bravado covering genuine terror. "Please, are you going to get me out? I feel like he's going to kill me any day now. The only time I'm allowed to leave his apartment is to come here, so nobody suspects something because I'm not at work."

"Are you sure he's not watching us right now?" Johnson said. "He's known to be very jealous. You meeting another man secretly... at work..."

Kennedy looked around, but like she was trying to avoid Johnson seeing her do it. "N-no, he said he had to take care of something tonight. A cleaning job."

"A cleaning job? Did you get the details? The DA is hoping to pin him for murder, after all."

"Whose murder?" Kennedy whispered.

"What was that?" Johnson asked.

"Whose. Murder." Kennedy's voice grew hard. "Because from where I'm standing, I'm pretty sure the victim is supposed to be me."

"We would never do that to you," her asshole handler said, trying to soothe her—probably for the sake of the wire *he* was wearing. "And for God's sake keep your voice down. You—"

I shot Kennedy in the stomach.

The Kevlar corset protected her, but the impact of it burst the blood pack we'd secured on the underside next to her skin. Blood slid down, dripping out from the bottom of the corset, staining her pelvis and legs, while also blooming across the fabric.

Kennedy gave a small, wheezing noise. *Don't move, baby girl, don't move.* I hit her again, higher up, in the chest.

Just like we'd planned, on the second hit she allowed herself to sink to the ground.

"Lancaster!?" Johnson sounded surprised. Shocked.

He probably thought I'd do this up close and in person, as was my trademark. That I'd wait and kill her later, after this conversation.

To his credit he knelt down to try and do CPR. The corset made it impossible for him to feel her heartbeat. Kennedy stared, open-eyed and blank-faced, up at the stars. She was damn good at playing dead.

"Shit," Johnson whispered. "Shit, she's dead."

He reached to check her pulse, and that just wouldn't do. He'd declared her dead to anyone listening in on their conversation, and it had to stay that way.

I raised the gun, aimed, and fired.

Headshot.

Johnson was dead the second the bullet hit his brain. He fell like a sack of bricks.

I couldn't hear the chatter, but I was certain the men listening in on the other end —the ones sitting in the fake taco truck van down the block—were losing their shit.

Two agents dead. They'd have no idea what to do with this.

I got down quickly from the roof as two of Jade's bouncers came out and retrieved Johnson's body. We'd deliver it to the DA's office in the morning. The time for subtlety was over.

Kennedy got to her feet, wobbling and pressing a hand to her stomach. "I know you said it would hurt, but that *hurt*."

"Yeah, fucking sucks." I grabbed her and pulled her in for a hug, fake blood and all. "You okay?"

"I am," Kennedy promised, even as she shook. "But I'll feel even better when—when we're away from all this."

"We will be," I promised her. "Very soon, we will be."

I held her, held her damn tightly, and let her fall apart in my arms. She wouldn't be alone anymore. Wouldn't be used anymore. This was my woman, the love of my goddamn life, and from now on, she had me and the protection of the Russo family.

She'd never feel like this again.

CHAPTER 24

Kennedy

The news was all over it.

A decorated member of the FBI was murdered by the same calling-card bullets used by a sniper employed by the Petrov family, one of Misha's crew. Of course the man had been murdered in the raid to rescue me, but that wasn't known to the general public. Vincent Russo had been smart enough not to mention his takedown of Misha and Co. until after I had 'died' and he made sure to frame it to anyone he spoke to as retaliation for my murder.

According to the press and the police, I had died a hero, murdered because I was Marco's girlfriend and only after death revealed to be a mole for the bureau.

The DA was fuming up one side and down the other, apparently. This was going to bring down a lot of heat—but on the Petrovs, not on us.

Not that the Petrovs had time to deal with this. In light of their 'blatant power-grab', to quote the spokesperson for the Wen family, the Petrovs had been undermining the work-force of the Chinese families in the city by giving them the funds to purchase their freedom from indentured servitude. *This is war,* the Chinese families vowed, and the Petrovs had their hands full.

Could they declare their innocence? All they wanted. But which was worse? Claiming the idea that they'd tried to grab more power, or admitting that they'd been used and duped, set up, made into patsies?

At least one of those options projected

strength and ambition, while the other only projected stupidity and slowness.

Marco was said to be publicly taking a vacation, somewhere warm and tropical, with beaches. He needed to get over the loss of his girlfriend, he said.

People rolled their eyes, certain he would have another girl on his arm soon enough. And he would.

Me.

My new name was Jackie. I thought it fitting, given my old name. I'd cut my hair short and dyed the strands to a soft auburn that Marco loved. I'd be a lovely vacationer that Marco met in the Bahamas and wooed into coming back to New York with him. With Kennedy Lancaster declared legally dead, murdered in front of witnesses—the Cozy Bunny bouncers—there was nothing the police could do even if they realized I was the same person and not just a woman who *looked* similar. The other families would probably know, of course. But that would be what Vincent and Marco wanted.

They would know the Russos had set up

the Petrovs, and that there was nothing the Petrovs could do to prove it.

More power to the Russos.

It was… easier than I thought to turn my back on my old life. I had nobody to say goodbye to. Nobody to really mourn me. And the anger of being used, set up, burned bright inside of me. One side of the law, I realized, was no better or worse than the other. And I knew which side loved me for myself and which side had tried to use me.

Marco found me out on the balcony of our hotel room on the third day of our trip, sunning myself on a lounge chair, on my stomach with my head resting on my arms. It was gorgeous here, and I felt like a lazy cat, soaking up as much sunlight as possible. It was glorious.

"Oh good, you're awake," I purred. I reached up and undid the tie of my bathing suit. "Want to rub sunscreen on my back? I think I missed a few spots."

Marco smirked at me and grabbed the bottle of sunscreen, kneeling down. "You're in a fine mood today, Miss Jacqueline."

I smiled as I felt his firm, broad hands

massaging my shoulders, my back, then skimming down against the sides of my breasts. "I'm in a fine mood every day, Mr. Russo."

"Insatiable," Marco murmured, his hands sliding lower and lower, moving around to my front.

I moaned and tilted my head to the side for a kiss. "Just like you," I whispered.

As his lips met mine, I knew I didn't regret any of my choices. This was where I belonged—with a man as wild as I was, a man with the same dark desires—the one man I could always trust. The one that only I could tame.

My wolf.

Don't miss Dante Russo's story, up next in RECKLESS SINNER!

For news and information on upcoming releases, please sign up for Erika Wilde's newsletter HERE.

All books in the MADE FOR THE MAFIA Series

Heartless Sinner

Ruthless Sinner

Reckless Sinner

* * *

To learn more about Erika Wilde and her upcoming releases, you can visit her at the following places on the web:

Website:

www.erikawilde.com

Facebook:

facebook.com/groups/erikawildesfanclub

Instagram:

https://www.instagram.com/erikawilde1/

Goodreads:

goodreads.com/erikawildeauthor

Made in the USA
Monee, IL
12 August 2025

22337709R00174